"You've got to get out of here!"

The scream of another incoming explosive buried Lillian's words, but thankfully, the blast struck farther away.

The man seemed to find his feet and trotted forward, his expression determined in spite of the blood that marred his face.

"You need to get to a hospital."

"No." He stopped, his earnest blue eyes boring into hers. "No hospital. I've got to get out of the country. I can't stay here. It's not safe." He took another step forward. "I have to hurry. Don't let them find me."

Lillian paused, unsure what she should do. It had always been her nature to help, to bind up injured animals, to rescue the wounded. That's why she'd gone to veterinary school. But she wavered now, uncertain whether she should try to help, or back off. She said a silent prayer that God would make clear what she was supposed to do.

Again the soldier's eyes met hers. "Help."

Books by Rachelle McCalla

Love Inspired Suspense

Survival Instinct
Troubled Waters
Out on a Limb
Danger on Her Doorstep
Dead Reckoning
*Princess in Peril
*Protecting the Princess
The Detective's Secret Daughter
*Prince Incognito

*Reclaiming the Crown

RACHELLE McCALLA

is a mild-mannered housewife, and the toughest she ever has to get is when she's trying to keep her four kids quiet in church. Though she often gets in over her head, as her characters do, and has to find a way out, her adventures have more to do with sorting out the carpool and providing food for the potluck. She's never been arrested, gotten in a fistfight or been shot at. And she'd like to keep it that way! For recipes, fun background notes on the places and characters in this book and more information on forthcoming titles, visit www.rachellemccalla.com.

PRINCE INCOGNITO

RACHELLE McCALLA

Love Inspired

PLEASE RECYCLE

THIS PRODUCT IS RECYCLABLE

Recycling programs
for this product may
not exist in your area.

™ LOVE INSPIRED BOOKS

ISBN-13: 978-0-373-67515-9

PRINCE INCOGNITO

Copyright © 2012 by Rachelle McCalla

www.LoveInspiredBooks.com

Printed in U.S.A.

"Whether you turn to the right or to the left,
your ears will hear a voice behind you saying,
'This is the way; walk in it.'"
—*Isaiah* 30:21

To Knox, my prince, with love.

ONE

His Royal Highness Prince Alexander of Lydia stood at attention in the palace courtyard, his back extra straight, his arms practically immobilized by the stiff sleeves of his dress uniform. The classic-cut olive-green suit was reserved for formal occasions, and Alec hadn't realized until he'd squeezed into it for this evening's state dinner just how long it had been since he'd last worn it.

About fifteen pounds of muscle ago, judging by how tight the shirt felt around his neck. He couldn't take a deep breath, and he felt a tingling sensation in his fingers every time he tried to bend his arms at the elbow. The warm weather of the June evening didn't help, though Alec was at least accustomed to heat.

His last deployment, a humanitarian mission in the deserts of North Africa, had required daily physical labor. Alec hadn't appreciated how much the work had transformed him until he'd returned home to Sardis, Lydia's capital city, the day before and found that none of his old clothes fit the same.

The limousines began to line up for the motorcade, and Alec watched his parents descend the palace steps with the rustle of sashes and silk. His father, His Majesty King Philip, waved Alec away from the head car.

"You'll be sixth in line." He pointed him farther down the queue.

"Why sixth? Who's in between us?" Though Alec didn't want to sound presumptuous, he was, after all, heir apparent to the throne of Lydia. While that didn't mean he had to ride in the front car, he certainly found it odd that he'd be placed so far down the line.

"State officials. Regional dignitaries. Guards."

"Guards?"

"Yes. Guards on motorcycles, guards in every car." King Philip motioned to a group of gun-bearing men. "You'll have one riding with you."

"A bodyguard?" Alec looked down at the young man who'd stepped forward. The kid wasn't small, but Alec was considerably larger, and he guessed, more experienced. "Father, I'm a soldier. I can take care of myself."

The king was halfway to his car, but as he looked back, he seemed to notice for the first time that his son had grown, and he deflated a little. "Fine. You can ride alone. But stay close. Stay safe." The king appeared as though he wanted to say more, but the cars and guards were waiting, and he ducked inside the limo after the queen.

Alec watched the door close after his parents, and their car rolled forward.

What was that all about? *Stay close? Stay safe?* Alec blinked at the abundance of men who filled the waiting vehicles and perched on their motorcycles, ready to go. Behind him, he spotted his sister Isabelle giving her bodyguard the cold shoulder as he held open the door to her waiting limousine. She'd told Alec that her request to have the guard removed had been turned down by their father.

Something strange was going on. When he'd first arrived home, Alec had assumed everything felt foreign simply because he wasn't used to it anymore. He'd acclimated to desert life, and no longer felt like he fit in with Lydia's aristocratic circles. In fact, until the announcement at tonight's dinner, when his father had promised he'd learn what his next assignment was, Alec didn't figure he'd feel as though he fit in anywhere.

But all the extra security, as well as his father's odd behavior, left Alec questioning what was going on. Sure, he was used to men with guns—but there weren't usually so many of them swarming the palace, were there? And whereas these events of state tended to be stressful for his father, today the king seemed downright jumpy.

Alec slid into his car, but he couldn't relax, in spite of the sumptuous leather seat of the limousine he was riding in. Too much about the situation bothered him.

Besides that, in a seated position, he could hardly take a breath.

His car crept forward, and Alec strained to see through the darkly tinted windows to the vehicles ahead of him. He hadn't seen any officials or dignitaries in the courtyard—no one had entered the vehicles ahead of him except for a few guards.

What was going on?

The motorcade progressed down the narrow streets of Sardis. Alec watched warily out the window, trying to sort out what had made his father, usually a self-assured ruler, act so skittish.

Crowds lined the sidewalks and people waved from balconies and open windows as the motorcade passed down the first few blocks. But the farther they went, the thinner the crowds became, and Alec craned his neck up ahead in time to spot uniformed men waving people inside.

More guards? Alec strained to see, but between the distance and the dark glass, he couldn't recognize their uniforms. Still, they looked like...

Lydian soldiers?

Alec lowered the window to get a better look. Without the sound of cheering crowds, he could hear the Lydian national anthem being projected from a low-fidelity speaker somewhere.

The window glass was a third of the way down when suddenly, it started moving up again.

Alec looked at the driver. Had he closed the window?

Rather than hit the intercom button to ask, Alec opened the door and stuck his head outside. As he squinted at the soldiers, the car slowed to a stop. Now what?

His father never allowed the royal motorcade to come to a complete stop. Had so much changed since Alec had been gone? Before he could sort it out, the uniformed men ahead of him shouted, leaping inside the nearest buildings.

Alec didn't have long to wonder at their actions. A dissonant, mechanical scream filled the air. Alec ducked behind the open door and pinched his eyes shut as a brilliant flash erupted in front of the motorcade's head car, its searing light penetrating his closed eyelids with its red glare. The moment it passed, Alec snapped his eyes open, following the grenade's trajectory upward to its source.

Two blocks ahead, he spotted a soldier on a high balcony, his assault rifle equipped with an under-barrel grenade launcher.

In the time it took the man to reload, Alec sized up the situation. Based on the sound and the blinding flash, he was nearly certain the soldier had shot a stun grenade—a sound-and light-emitting device designed to incapacitate targets by causing immediate but temporary deafness and flash-blindness. The weapon was technically classified as nonlethal, but only when used in an environment free of combustibles.

Given the number of vehicles in the motorcade, and the likelihood they were all carrying full tanks of fuel, the diversion grenade could be plenty lethal. Immediately Alec feared for the safety of his sisters traveling in the limousines behind his.

Before the soldier got his weapon raised again, Alec made his decision. The royal limousines were lightweight-armor plated. For budget reasons, King Philip had never deemed it necessary to commission defensive countermeasures or military-grade armor. The car would offer little protection against a stun grenade—and Alec had no guarantee that's all the soldier would be shooting. If a fragmentation grenade struck the motorcade, it could kill everyone in a ten-meter radius.

Rather than wait to find out what the soldier had used to reload, Alec sprinted for the cars behind him, where his sisters were. He had to reach them, to help them find cover before the blasts became deadly. Stun grenades were a tactical weapon, often used for clearing the way for the big guns. He might not have much time!

A squeal rent the air above his head an instant before another stun grenade hit the rear of the motorcade, spewing thick smoke for dozens of meters in every direction. Was this what his father had been nervous about? Had the king somehow gotten wind that an attack was being planned? Had the royal family been specifically targeted?

Alec could see no sign of his sisters—he could hardly see the *cars* through the heavy smoke. He prayed for their safety as he staggered forward, uncertain whether he was even still heading in the right direction, disoriented by the eruptions. Isabelle had been wary of the bodyguard who'd been appointed to protect her, and Stasi… Come to think of it, he hadn't even seen Stasi.

Another deafening squeal filled the air, the sound tearing at his ears as it approached, closer this time. Alec flung himself backward instinctively, diving away from the eruption, praying for some form of cover.

Heat swelled behind him as he felt the stone of a limestone wall. A building! He turned away from it, pushing himself back into the heat and smoke and chaos. His sisters were back there. He had to reach them. He had to find them!

His ears throbbed, too traumatized to hear, but he felt the vibrations of the next incoming eruption, closer this time, and more powerful. He spun around, bracing himself to run, to dive toward his sisters' cars, but there was no time. The concussion caught him before his feet hit the ground, propelling him sideways, the shock wave pulsing through him like an electrical fire.

Then all was black, and silent.

The ringing in his ears began slowly, and Alec peeled his face away from the weathered limestone, blinking as his eyes focused on a red smear across the cream-colored stones.

Why was there blood on the stones?

He looked down. Blood splashed against his suit. Where was he? What was happening?

Stumbling forward, he tried to remember.

He'd been attacked, surrounded.

He had to escape.

He had to survive.

Lillian Bardici turned and ran down the alley for her rented rickshaw as the sound of another blast erupted, nearer this time. Heat from the blast sizzled down the alleyway, swelling past her as she ran. Okay, so maybe watching the royal motorcade pass by *hadn't* been such a good idea. Maybe she should have listened to her parents, who wanted to set sail earlier in the afternoon. They could have been in the middle of the Mediterranean by now, far from the explosions on the street behind her.

Glancing back over her shoulder, Lily saw a man in an olive soldier's uniform—different from those of the officers who'd waved her back from the street. He'd barely made it to the opening of the alleyway when another blast struck.

Lily ducked back into the thick stone archway of a limestone doorway. Waves of heat plunged past her, and she caught her breath, praying.

Dear God, help me! Help that soldier!

Her heart pinched at the thought of the handsome man who'd had no chance to escape the blast. As soon as the first swell passed by, Lillian peeked out.

The soldier leaned against the wall, a red streak of blood painting the creamy limestone behind him, marking the place where his face had grated against the wall. He raised his head just as she looked at him, and she saw disorientation in his eyes. He staggered forward a few steps.

Lillian couldn't leave him. If another blast hit, he'd be done for. She ran forward. "Hurry. You've got to get out of here!" The scream of another incoming explosive buried her words, but thankfully, the blast struck farther away. Though it shook the ground beneath them, she felt none of its heat.

The man seemed to find his feet and trotted forward, his expression determined in spite of the blood that marred the left half of his face.

"Can I help you?" Lily asked as he reached her.

She stumbled along beside him. "You need to get to a hospital."

"No." He stopped, his earnest blue eyes boring into hers. "No hospital. I've got to get out of the country. It's not safe here." He took another step forward. "Hurry. Don't let them find me."

"Don't let *who* find you?"

Another distant blast erupted, and the soldier plodded past her, toward her rickshaw that sat at the end of the alley. Lily caught up to him just as he paused next to it.

Again, his eyes met hers. "Help."

Unsure what he meant, Lily reached for his arm, steadying him as he sagged into the back passenger seat of her tricycle-like rented rickshaw.

She looked at him for only a second, his eyes closed, his body slumped down. From her medical training, Lillian knew the concussive shock waves from explosions could cause tremendous internal injuries, often with no external harm. The damage was likely catching up to him already.

Goaded on by the eruptions behind them, Lily hopped onto the bike and pointed the handlebars downhill. Between the added weight of the soldier behind her and the downward slope of the streets as the city gave way to the sea, she had no trouble getting her bike moving.

The marina was a mere three blocks away, all downhill. Her parents had already said they wanted to cast off that afternoon, but Lillian had begged them to stay long enough for her to watch the motorcade pass by. Her father hadn't been happy about it, insisting that they should leave before the state dinner. But when she'd pointed out all the other promises he'd broken in the past few weeks, he had reluctantly agreed. She'd promised to return immediately thereafter, and return the rickshaw at the stand at the head of the pier. They could leave immediately.

Since she'd personally run all their errands while they'd been in port in Sardis, renting the bike so she could haul fresh stores of food and water, it had seemed only fair that she be allowed to stay a little longer. And she'd promised they could be gone before the state dinner began.

Now Lillian questioned the wisdom of her decision as the rickshaw picked up speed, careening toward the pier. She laid on the brakes as she blew past the rickshaw rental stand, and just managed to skid to a stop next to her parents' yacht.

"Lillian!" Her mother, Sandra, gasped when she saw the soldier's bloody form slumped on the back of her bike.

Her father's jaw dropped.

But by the time he found his voice to insist that Lily take the soldier right back to where she'd found him, Lillian had already dismounted from the bike. The rail of their yacht bobbed a little higher than the dock, but the bike sat higher still. Lily tipped the rickshaw, and the unconscious soldier keeled toward the cushioned bench that encircled the deck of the yacht.

"Lily, no!" Michael Bardici demanded, rushing forward to stop her, an instant too late.

With a hefty heave, the soldier tumbled gracelessly onto the cushion. Lily hopped onboard after him, rearranging his arms and legs to settle him flat on his back.

"Lily." Her mother approached, wringing her hands. "Did you see what was going on up there? It's like a war zone."

"Mom, please. Can you push the rickshaw back up the pier? We have to get out of town."

Her mother paused, surprise on her face, then obediently climbed onto the dock and took the bike back up to the rental stand.

Lifting the man's eyelids to check his pupils for signs of concussion, Lillian listened with one ear to her father's protests.

"What are you thinking bringing that man onboard? There's been some sort of violent attack up there, and now you're getting us mixed up in it. What will your uncle David say?"

Lily focused on her examination and didn't respond. The man's pupils were even, with no telltale red streaks that would have indicated his capillaries had burst. A good sign. Hopefully the alleyway had blocked much of the force of the blast, preventing a traumatic concussion. It boded well for the likelihood of minimal internal injuries.

Her father inserted his face in her line of sight. "I know you think you have to rescue every injured creature that crosses your path, but this is going too far. He's a human being. You can't take him out of his country—"

"He asked me to take him out of the country."

"Oh, he did, did he?"

"Yes." She checked the soldier's pulse. Strong. "He specifically asked me to help him, to get him out of the country, and to hurry."

"Did he say anything else?"

She looked her father full in the face. "Don't let them find me."

"Who's he hiding from?" Michael Bardici sputtered. "Did he have something to do with those explosions? He could be a criminal!"

Before Lily could respond, her mother returned. "Let's *do* hurry and get out of here," Sandra Bardici requested. "There are soldiers with guns everywhere. Whatever those explosions were about, I don't like it. What if they try to lock down the marina?"

Lily felt grateful her mother had so quickly sized up the situation. "She's right, Dad. We should get moving. Do you need me to help you get under sail, or can I bandage his face?"

"You should do nothing of the sort," her father protested. "Surely there's somewhere in the city." He looked at Sardis beyond the bay, black smoke rising above the limestone buildings, and his protest lost a little power.

"We should get out of the marina while we still can." Sandra sounded almost frantic.

"Of course we should go." Michael Bardici faced his wife. "But we can't take this man with us! We don't know anything about him. What if he's dangerous?"

"He looks to be out cold right now. She's brought him this far. It's chaos up there—I suppose the local hospital will be overwhelmed. She's a trained medical professional."

"She just graduated from *veterinary* school."

Sandra took a step closer to her husband and lowered her voice. "She wants to help. This is the first time she's wanted to do anything medical since…"

Lily heard her mother's sentence hang in the air, and knew exactly what words she hadn't spoken. Since she'd failed to save the horses. The painful memory taunted her, but she pushed it away. Thinking about the tragedy in her past wasn't going to help her now.

Michael Bardici huffed. "Fine. We'll set sail. But I'll warn you both—I intend to get rid of this fellow at the first opportunity." He stomped over and untied the boat.

"Thank you, Dad." Lily sprinted into the top-level pilothouse and pulled out the first-aid kit, which she had personally assembled in a small suitcase years before, and kept stocked for emergencies.

The unconscious soldier didn't flinch as she cleaned the wound on his face. To her relief, the abrasions didn't appear to be deep, though they stretched from his nose to his ear, covering much of his forehead, down to his chin. Still, if she bandaged his face quickly and kept the injuries clean, he'd likely heal with minimal scarring.

Once she had the blood cleaned off and a fresh white bandage wrapped around his head to hold the gauze and batting in place, she pulled out her otoscope and checked his ears, sighing with relief when she saw no sign of blood.

Excellent. Ears were particularly susceptible to primary-blast injuries. The fact that they'd sustained no damage reduced the likelihood that he'd been hit with enough concussive force to injure his lungs or his brain. She'd heard horror stories of those with blast-force injuries to the brain who'd lost their memories, and developed short tempers as well as ongoing headaches. Only time would tell the extent of the soldier's injuries, but for the time being, Lillian's hopes were buoyed by her discovery.

With her attention focused on the soldier, she hardly noticed the progress of their 52-foot vessel as they left the marina and reached the open sea.

"Did you want something to eat, Lily?" Her mother climbed up from the below-deck cabins and handed her a bottle of water.

Surprised, Lily realized the sun had already sunk low on the horizon. "No, thank you. Water's fine."

Her mother sat on the bench near the man's feet. "Your father's very upset."

Lily gestured to the soldier as she placed her otoscope back in its case. "He asked me to help."

"I know. And I'm glad you want to help again. But he's not an injured animal. He's a person."

"Doesn't that make him even more worthy of my help?"

Her mother sighed.

Lily changed the subject. "Can you help me try to get him out of his suit jacket? There's blood on his shirt. I just want to make sure it came from his face. I don't want to miss an injury."

Her mother agreed, propping up the soldier's torso while Lily tugged the suit jacket off his arms. She wasn't sure if it was the humidity or a sizing issue, but the jacket didn't want to come off. The soldier had been wearing a dark olive dress uniform—maybe he'd been en route to the state dinner. His choice of apparel certainly seemed too formal for an ambush attack. A cluster of medals decorated the garment at the chest, topped by a badge bearing one name. "Lydia."

When Lillian finally pulled the man's arms free, Sandra ran her fingers over the name as she folded the jacket neatly. "What do you suppose this means?" She held out the badge for Lily to see.

Lily was already working on the soldier's shirt buttons, praying silently that he'd be okay. If a shrapnel wound snuck past her, the soldier could bleed out overnight. "Lydia is the name of the country."

"But the other soldiers we saw in Lydia didn't have the name of the country on their badge. They had their last names."

Lily tried to think. If she was honest with herself, she felt uncomfortable checking the soldier's chest for injuries because he was attractive—wounded or not. "Maybe Lydia is his last name, then."

"Why would his last name be the same as the name of his country?"

"I don't know." Lily focused her attention on inspecting the man in the dying evening light. One thing was for certain—he'd been in fine physical shape before the attack. Lily felt herself blush as she checked his torso for any sign that shrapnel might have penetrated his uniform. Cleaning off the residual blood on his chest, she determined it had soaked through from the outside, no doubt originating from the injuries to his face.

"Did he tell you his name?"

"There wasn't time to ask." Lillian reached for the man's side pants pocket, where a squarish bulge indicated something was stowed. "Maybe he has some ID on him." She pulled out the contents of his pocket—a wad of unfamiliar bills, secured with a pewter money clip.

"Those aren't euros," her mom observed.

"I don't know what they are." Lillian flipped through the banknotes, looking for anything that would indicate which country they originated from.

"Why would a Lydian soldier be carrying foreign currency?" Sandra Bardici mused aloud.

Lillian wondered the same thing. Lydia, a small Christian kingdom squeezed along the shoreline between Albania and Greece, traded in euros, the official currency of most of Europe. "It does seem a little odd." She shook off a shiver.

"Do you suppose he's working for a foreign nation? He might have been part of the group that staged that attack."

"I don't know. We'll have to wait for him to wake up so we can ask him." Lily stuffed the money back into the soldier's pocket. Satisfied that she'd done all she could for him, she watched his chest rise and fall. He seemed to be breathing easier without the restrictive suit. From what she'd observed, she guessed he wasn't terribly old, maybe mid-to late-twenties, hardly any older than she was. And in spite of the bandage covering half his face, he was handsome, with sandy brown hair in a military cut, and a strong, square jaw.

Her mother had given up her inquiries. "Don't put his bloody shirt back on him. I'll get him one of your father's old T-shirts." She retreated back into the cabin, and Lily could hear her footsteps carry her below deck.

As she lowered the man from his propped-up position, Lily's hands grazed something rough on his back. Afraid she might have missed an injury in the fading light, she traced the ridge with her fingers, then propped him up higher to get a better look.

A network of healing scabs crisscrossed his back, as though he'd been beaten or whipped. As Lily surveyed the extent of the damage, her sympathy for the soldier increased even as she wondered what had caused the marks. It reminded her of the horrors of slavery, and yet, even this far from America, she couldn't imagine the man having been enslaved, not in the twenty-first century.

She thought of the uniform jacket her mother had carried downstairs. The man was a soldier. "Were you a prisoner of war?" She voiced the question in a whisper, not expecting a response.

Settling the man's torso back gently onto the cushion, Lily let his head rest on her lap for just a second as she held the edge of the boat, preparing to scoot out from under him.

The man moaned and shifted his head.

Lily froze. She'd been thinking that he ought to drink something, but she didn't want to shove it down his throat and risk drowning him. She figured if he was reviving, however slightly, now was her chance. She grabbed the water bottle her mother had brought her.

A dark blanket of pain settled heavily across his face. He wanted to push it away, but it felt so heavy, and his mouth was dry. So dry.

"Water?"

The word came from somewhere beyond him, a gentle, feminine voice.

"Can you sit up a little and drink?"

Who was this creature who knew exactly what he longed for? She'd soothed the pain on his face. She had water. He tried to obey her instructions, to lift his head.

He opened his mouth. Couldn't she just pour it down his throat? He couldn't see. There was too much darkness, and too much pain. His head throbbed.

"Can you swallow?"

Something touched his lips, and he felt a tiny

pool of cool liquid. "More." He tried to speak, but it came out as a groan.

"Here—slowly."

He gulped too much, and sputtered. Afraid the woman would remove the water before his thirst was remotely quenched, he felt relieved when the bottle touched his lips again. He focused on each cool swallow that soothed his parched tongue and dry throat.

Then the water was gone, and he moaned, wanting it back.

"You've got to have a horrible headache." Gentle fingers touched his forehead. "Can you swallow a pill? It will help with the pain."

If the woman with the water could make his headache go away, he would know God had sent her. He tried to answer, to nod—anything—but the blanket was too heavy for him to push past. Gratitude swelled within him as he felt her place something just inside his mouth.

And then more water. Ah, sweet water. He swallowed it greedily until the bottle held no more.

"That's enough for now. We don't know if you've sustained any internal injuries, and we don't want to overwhelm them."

The gentle voice hinted at something. Injuries? That would explain the pain. Who was this gentle woman who eased his pain?

Come to think of it, who was he? Fighting back

against the throbbing in his head, he tried to think, but the pain only pounded louder, the blanket of darkness heavier. He tried for a moment to resist it, then gave in to its pressing darkness.

TWO

Lillian left the soldier sleeping on the cushioned bench and headed for the pilothouse, where her father was bound to be sulking at the wheel, resenting her for rescuing the man. After helping her squeeze the soldier into an old T-shirt, her mother had gone belowdecks, where the 52-foot sloop housed three cabins, two bathrooms and the freshly stocked kitchen. Night had fallen, and Lily knew her mother was tired from the events of the day. No doubt she'd gone on to bed.

Padding silently up the steps to the pilothouse, Lily heard her father's voice and realized he was on the phone. Not wanting to interrupt him, she held back, trying to evaluate how long he might spend on the call.

"Ha! I wish it had been a dolphin. I'd even take a shark. No, this time she rescued a human. What's that? Yes, you heard right. A person. A soldier, actually. He was injured in all those explosions. Now he's passed out on deck with some sort of concussion."

Lily listened intently, hoping to discern how upset her father really was about her new project.

"If he has a name, I haven't heard what it is. His uniform said *Lydia.* Yes, right above his medals, like it was his last name."

Heart thudding hard, Lily wondered if her father might learn something that would help identify the man she'd rescued. She and her parents had sailed to Lydia to visit her uncle David, who was a general in charge of the Lydian Army. If that was who her father was speaking to, he might well know their mystery soldier's identity.

Her father sucked in a breath. "But, Dave, we're already twenty miles out to sea, and he's unconscious. If I throw him overboard, he'll drown."

Lily clutched the doorframe and ducked back, suddenly aware that her innocent intentions had turned into serious eavesdropping. Her uncle David wanted the soldier tossed overboard? Surely her father would talk him out of it.

"I understand. Yes, yes, I see your point. I don't know much about those kinds of injuries myself, but we don't want him lingering for days just to die on our boat. No, she didn't have any luck with the horses, and she's still torn up about that. I suppose it's better this way."

What? Was her father actually planning to push

the man overboard? He'd die for sure! Lily tried to think. Her father was upset with her for rescuing the soldier in the first place. She'd overreached his favor already, so there would be little use begging him to change his mind. Besides, she'd learned over the course of their visit to Lydia that her father's older brother had tremendous influence over her dad—far more than she had.

As Michael Bardici went on about the soldier's injuries, and his fears that the soldier might awaken in a terrible rage and murder them all in their sleep, Lily tiptoed back to the injured man's side. He'd roused earlier, when he'd taken the pain relievers she'd given him. If those had gone to work, maybe she could wake him up all the way. He'd have to defend himself against her father. She didn't see any other way out of the situation.

Crouching by his side, she patted his uninjured cheek. "Excuse me, sir? You've got to wake up!" He emitted a low moan, but didn't move. She shook his shoulders. If she could just rouse him, surely the strong soldier would be able to ward off her father, even in his injured state.

"Please—you've got to wake up." She bent close to his ear. "My father wants to toss you overboard. We're way out into the Mediterranean. There's nowhere to go if you go overboard. You've got to wake up!" She shook him hard, her alarm increasing as she heard footsteps crossing the deck behind her.

"Lillian." Michael Bardici's voice was stern. "What are you doing?"

She turned to confront him, not caring if desperation showed on her face. "This man is under my protection." She wished her voice wouldn't tremble.

"He's injured. He probably won't live more than a couple of days. Your uncle explained to me about these blast injuries. They explode a person from the inside—"

"His ears were fine. That means the impact of the blast wasn't strong enough to cause internal injuries."

"Then why won't he wake up?"

Lily groaned. The man behind her on the bench was rousing. She'd watched his eyelids flutter. Given another minute, he might be able to pull himself from his pain-filled sleep. *If* she could buy him another minute.

Backing against the bench, she spread her arms wide as though to physically block Michael Bardici from reaching the prone soldier. "He's recovering. He just needs time."

"And then what? He'll awaken in a fit of terror and kill us all."

"No, he won't."

"You don't know that. You don't know him.

Your uncle David recognized the name from his uniform. He was part of the insurgent uprising that caused all that commotion in Sardis. Don't you see, Lillian? We can't trust him. He's dangerous."

"He's a human being. If you toss him overboard, he'll die. That's called murder, and it's illegal." She didn't bother to mention that it went against the Bible's teachings. Her father didn't share her faith, and she'd learned not to try to foist it on him.

"It's not illegal if it's done in self-defense."

"He's not threatening you."

"Not now, but if he wakes up and tries something, he could overpower all three of us. Besides, if I don't do it, David said he'd drop everything and take care of the man himself. You saw the explosions in town. Your uncle has his hands full. He shouldn't have to come out here and clean up the mess I never should have let you make in the first place." The words sounded more like something her uncle David would say, and Lily realized her father was likely quoting his older brother. "One little push, Lily. That's all it will take." He advanced slowly until he was less than an arm's length away.

Lily could feel the tears streaming down her cheeks, and the rising helplessness that had overcome her when her father's horses had begun to die. She would have done anything to save the horses, but there had been nothing she could do.

She wasn't going to let it happen again, especially not to a human being. "You *can't.* You just can't. We'll put in at the next port and I'll leave him off there. I don't care where it is. Find me a beach somewhere, and I promise I'll leave him, but you can't just push him over in the middle of the sea."

Even as she spoke, begging for her father's mercy, his expression hardened. He reached past her, getting his hands under the soldier's shoulders.

"No! You can't!" She tried to pry his arm away. The soldier groaned and blinked. He was waking up!

But he was too late.

Her father shoved his shoulder between her and the half-conscious soldier, scooping his arm under him, tilting him toward the rail.

"No!" Lily held the soldier's shoulders, fighting to keep him on the boat.

"Let go." Michael pulled her hands free and got an arm under the man's torso, leveraging him up even as the awakening man grasped the air in front of him.

"Don't do it!" Lily pounced atop the bench, throwing all her weight into the tug-of-war.

Her mother gasped from the direction of the below-deck stairs. "Lily! What are you doing?"

Startled, Lily looked up just as her father caught

her by her shoulders, plucking her up and tossing her back toward her mother. She scrambled back, shocked by her father's behavior. He'd thrown her across the boat! She found her feet as her father got his arms under the soldier and, with one giant heave, tossed him over the side.

"No!" Lily screamed as she leapt across the deck. Kicking off her sneakers, she bounded onto the bench and leapt over the rail, diving into the Mediterranean water. A moment later she rose and looked frantically about. The sea was fairly calm, but they'd been cutting through the water at a good clip, and had no doubt passed the spot where the soldier had gone overboard.

Spotting something white—his T-shirt, perhaps—she kicked her legs out and swam toward it, just as her mother's screams carried through the air, and a life preserver flew past her head, its rope unfurling behind it.

The rope splashed across her just as her right leg kicked down, catching the cord in a tangle. For one terrified instant, she realized it had twined around her leg. Then the dogged progress of the boat through the water pulled the line taught, dragging her backward with it. She tried to scream, to gulp a breath, anything, but the overwhelming force pulled her through the sea, poring water into her nose, her eyes, her mouth.

She tried to reach the rope to untangle it, but the

press of the water was far too great for her to fight against. With sinking terror, she realized there was nothing she could do to free herself. The sun had set and the night was dark. Would her parents even be able to see what had happened? Even if they quickly realized they needed to haul her in, by the time they got the boat stopped, she'd likely be drowned.

Shock rippled through him as he hit the water, snapping him into the full consciousness that had evaded him as he'd tried to pull himself from sleep moments before. Where was he? What had happened? Acting on instinct, he clawed upward for air, and saw the stars twinkling down from the night sky above.

A scream caught his attention, and he saw a woman throw a life preserver. It fell just short of him, and he cleared the distance to it in a couple of strokes. Grabbing hold, he got his head up enough above the water to see.

There were arms in the water.

No, more than arms, there was a woman. Her leg was caught on the rope to his life preserver, and the moving boat hauled her backward through the water, facedown, helpless.

He recognized her brown hair, her pale pink top. He'd glimpsed her before through pain-dulled eyes. It was the woman who'd given him water and made his pain go away!

Pulling on the rope, he hauled her toward him, and looped one arm under her torso. Gently, he lifted her up and shoved the flotation device under her head. He peeled back the long brown hair and found her face just as she gasped a breath and belched up seawater.

"Can you hold the ring?"

She coughed, but clutched the flotation device with white-knuckled fingers.

"Hold tight." He knew he had to get her leg untangled, or risk her being pulled back under again. Fighting the current created by the moving boat that tugged them relentlessly forward, he pulled himself along the loose length of rope, caught hold of where it had pulled taught, and held it behind her, creating enough slack to allow him to squeeze it back past her heel, and work her foot free.

He dropped her foot and swam back to her head, balancing himself above the life preserver, level with her eyes. "Are you okay?"

She coughed and looked like she was trying to nod.

He peeled back more of the sodden hair that covered her face. She really was beautiful, even half drowned.

Whoever was running the boat had gotten it

slowed down considerably, and voices were yelling something, but he couldn't make out what.

"Here." He eased the woman onto his shoulder as he held tight to the rope. "I'm going to pull us up."

She clung to him, her head slumped against his neck, her rattling breath easing as she tightened her grip on his shoulders. "Stairs," she said, and coughed again. "Stairs—at the stern."

He didn't doubt there were stairs at the back of the boat, but he wasn't about to let go of the rope to go looking for them. The night was too dark, the sea too vast and the boat was still cutting through the water, though more slowly now.

"I've got you. Just hold on tight." Pulling hand-over-hand up the rope, he moved them closer to the boat, until he kicked the hull with his boots and fairly walked up the side, rappelling against the sailboat.

The woman clutched him tighter as they rose out of the water and the ship tipped slightly from their combined weight.

"Can you climb aboard?" he asked the woman as he got one hand on the rail.

"No. You first," she whispered. "If I get on-board, he'll only push you over again."

Unsure of whom the woman referred to, he nonetheless heaved one shoulder over the rail.

Hands pulled at the woman in his arms, but she

held on to him tightly as he rolled them both over the railing and scrambled to standing on the deck.

"Lily." An older woman reached for the girl he'd rescued, but she shook her head and shoved him toward a doorway that led down stairs to the lit cabins belowdecks. He obediently headed in the direction he was pushed.

"Lillian." A man stepped in front of them, barring the way.

"He can have my room." The waterlogged young woman pleaded, her voice trembling. "Let him be. We can leave him at the next port."

But the man looked angry, and regarded him with a scowl.

Straightening to his full height, he returned the man's glare. He couldn't remember who he was, but he was nearly certain he could take the older man if it came to a fight.

The man must have realized it, too, because he stepped aside, his mouth set in a grim line.

She pushed him ahead of her, down the stairs, and guided him into a comfortable-looking full-size berth and en-suite bathroom.

He spotted a waterproof chair and slumped down on it.

"Lily?" The older woman was at the door again. "What are you thinking, letting that man in your room?"

"He's too big for the guest room. And this way,

he'll have his own private bathroom." Lily left the door open a crack and addressed her through the gap. "I'm just going to re-dress his bandages. I'll move to the guest room for tonight."

"Fine." The woman shrank away with a resigned sigh, and Lily closed the door.

He caught his breath as Lily approached him, her movements cautious.

"Do you mind if I remove your bandages?"

"Please." He sat still as she peeled the soaking wet red-stained gauze from his head.

"I need to run upstairs and get the first-aid kit. I'll be right back. If you feel light-headed, you can lie down." She disappeared, and returned quickly with a suitcase-size first-aid kit. Perching on the edge of the bed beside his chair, she gingerly dabbed his face with ointment, her touch gentle.

"Your name is Lily?" He repeated the name he'd heard the other woman use.

"Lillian Bardici."

He tried to think. *Bardici.* It sounded vaguely familiar, but he couldn't place it. But then, he didn't even know who he was. Everything had happened so quickly, and he had far more questions than answers. "Do you know who I am?"

"No. Don't you remember?"

He closed his eyes and tried to think, but the throbbing in his head drowned out all his thoughts. "I don't. The last thing I can recall is being thirsty, and you gave me a drink. How did we end up in the water?"

"My father threw you overboard. I jumped in after you."

"To rescue me?" He couldn't imagine that the slender woman would have had much success dragging him aboard if he hadn't awakened, but at the same time, he felt grateful that she'd tried.

"Yes." She squeezed more antibacterial ointment from a tube. "To try, anyway."

"Why did your father throw me over?"

"It's kind of a long story." Lillian sighed as her gentle hands eased the salt-sting on his wounds. "My parents and I have been living on this boat for the past month—that's a long story, too. We sailed from New York to Lydia to visit my father's older brother, David. He's a general in the Lydian Army. I don't like my uncle at all. He's extremely bossy, and he pushes my dad around. My uncle told my parents that we needed to leave Lydia before the state dinner tonight."

"Why?"

"I don't know." Lillian wiped ointment from her fingers onto a towel before trimming a length of clean gauze to cover his injury. "At the time, I just thought he was being controlling. But maybe he had some inkling about what was going to happen." She looked at him thoughtfully.

He studied her face, trying to read what she

was thinking. Her blue eyes were streaked with pale gray and green, giving them an almost aquamarine undertone, stunningly beautiful, like the Mediterranean Sea.

Lillian shrugged and continued her story. "I wanted to see the royal motorcade pass by. The kingdom of Lydia has a royal family, but news about them rarely reaches the United States. I've seen pictures of the princesses—they're so elegant, and always promoting humanitarian causes—but the rest of the royal family is fairly private. I just wanted to catch a glimpse…"

"Did you?"

"Hardly. Soldiers pushed everyone back, and then explosions started going off everywhere. I was afraid we'd all be killed."

Explosions, yes. He pinched his eyes shut, shadows of memories taunting him from beyond the pain-filled recesses of his mind. Slivers of memories fell down like dust motes shaken free. "They were diversion grenades—classified as nonlethal."

"What? You remember?" She looked startled, maybe even frightened. "How do you know that?"

But the memory melted away like a snowflake in the sun, evaporating to nothingness even as he reached for it. "I don't know how I know." He shook his head, wishing he could as easily shake loose the thoughts held prisoner inside. He sighed. "That might explain why I can't remember much—the trauma from the blast must have temporarily wiped out my memory."

"Temporarily." Lillian repeated. "How soon do you think it will be before you get it back?"

"Hard to say. Hopefully not long. Stun grenades aren't mean to inflict permanent damage."

"How is it that you know that, but you don't remember your own name?"

He thought carefully before answering. "I remember how to speak. I remember how to swim."

"I'm grateful you remembered that much." Her small smile seemed intended to encourage him.

It warmed his heart. He wished, for her sake, that he could remember. That he had answers to give her. She'd already helped him so much, and he'd done nothing but get her in trouble. "The concussion may have only affected one area of my brain—my personal memories. Hopefully the blast wasn't too strong, and I'll recover my memory soon."

"Maybe that explains why you weren't injured any worse than you were." Lillian taped a bandage securely into place. "Whatever those explosions were, I thought for sure we'd all be killed. I saw you in an alley, and ran for my bike just as you did. When you climbed in the backseat I pedaled for the yacht, dumped you onboard, and we got away from Sardis as quickly as we could. *But—*"

she took a deep breath "—my father talked to my uncle, who told him to throw you overboard."

"Why?"

"He said you're dangerous." Lillian sat back, her hands on her knees as she leaned away from him as though she thought he might be dangerous, too.

"Dangerous?" He mulled over the thought.

"My uncle said you were involved with the insurgents who ambushed the royal motorcade." Her voice grew thoughtful. "You knew what kind of grenades they were shooting."

Sensing the uncertainty Lillian struggled with, he scrambled to think of something reassuring he could tell her. But everything beyond the last ten minutes was covered by a dark cloud, and the circumstances she'd found him in certainly sounded suspicious. "Do you think I'm dangerous?"

She let out a breath and blinked at the floor, finally meeting his eyes again. "I don't know."

Hope flirted with the doubt in her eyes. She wanted to trust him. He wanted to be worthy of that trust, but he didn't know enough about his own history to know if he was. "So why are you helping me?"

"You were injured. You asked me to help you—to get you out of Lydia before they found you."

"Before who found me?"

"I suppose it depends on whose side you're on." She gave him that wary, uncertain look again.

He wanted to assure her that he was a person of integrity and honor, not someone to be feared, but he couldn't claim something he didn't know to be true. The unknowns of his past sat between them like a live grenade that might go off at any moment.

Lillian rose to her feet. "Do you need anything? There's drinking water there, and a few snacks." She pointed to a small fridge that served as a nightstand. "Help yourself."

Her hospitality surprised him. She didn't know whether he could be trusted, and yet, she'd given up her room for him, and had gone out of her way to make him comfortable.

Lillian stopped halfway to the door. "I'll be across the hall if you need anything. You might want to lock yourself in the room. Don't trust my father."

"Thank you." He took a step forward, intending to shake her hand.

She shrank back against the door frame.

"I have no intention of hurting you." He assured her quickly, wishing he had evidence to back up his claim. "I don't think I'm dangerous."

Her eyes flickered across the breadth of his shoulders, to the thick biceps that stretched the sleeves of the T-shirt he wore, up to his full height, towering over her in the close confines of the stateroom. "I think—" a tremor cut through her words "—you could be plenty dangerous, if you wanted to be."

He lowered his head. She had an excellent point. His powerful physique indicated that he lived a lifestyle that required him to be strong. Did that mean he was dangerous? Her uncle and her father thought so.

"Thank you for everything—" he began, startled by the sound of someone knocking on the other side of the heavily lacquered mahogany door.

Lillian looked concerned and stepped away from the door to make room to open it.

As she did so, the door swung open, virtually eliminating any open floor space in the tiny room. He shrank back, intending to get out of her way, but she must have had the same thought, because she stumbled into him and he reached out to steady her just as the door swung open.

Lily's father stood on the other side, his face red up to his receding hairline, his eyes bulging with anger.

Lily shuffled away, but the move only made her look that much more guilty as she disentangled herself from his arms.

"Lillian," her father seethed. "What are you doing?"

She opened her mouth to answer.

He raised one hand, silencing her as he addressed the soldier. "Who are you?"

"I don't know," he admitted.

"He's lost his memory from the blasts," Lily explained. "But he could regain it at any time."

Lily's father shook his head. "It doesn't matter. This man is coming with me."

"Why? Where?" Lillian looked as though she might try to step between them.

"Your uncle David would like to see him." Her father grabbed the soldier by his arm. "On deck. Now."

He could have fought the older man, but having just assured Lillian that he wasn't dangerous, he didn't figure he ought to strike her father. That left him with no choice but to walk in the direction he was shoved.

"Stay in your room, Lily."

"No." The stubborn woman trailed them both up onto the deck.

For one disorientated moment, he thought perhaps a storm had blown up. Then he recognized the familiar sound of a military helicopter's pulsing rotors.

He tensed, all his instincts telling him there was danger in the darkness.

A man stepped into the dim circle of light provided by a fixture next to the pilothouse door. Other than the military uniform he wore, and his hair more salt than pepper, he looked like Lillian's father.

The uniformed man—apparently Lily's uncle David—spoke. "You tried to run away. That was foolish." He raised a hand, gesturing to somewhere beyond them.

Four uniformed men stepped from the shadows—soldiers, with guns slung across their backs. They stepped toward him as though to apprehend him.

His heart pounded. Should he fight them or go nicely? He didn't even know who he was—how was he supposed to know how to respond to these men?

"No!" Lillian screamed from behind him, pushing her way between him and the men who approached.

The soldiers reacted, two of them lunging toward him, two others rushing her, intention to harm spelled across their features and their postures.

He made up his mind instantly. He couldn't let them hurt Lillian.

Whipping his boot around in a high-round kick, he sent the nearest two soldiers sprawling.

THREE

Lillian staggered back, as the soldier who'd rescued her from the sea dispatched a flurry of kicks at the soldiers who swarmed the deck of her father's sloop. The first two fell and didn't rise. He disarmed the next, pulling the intimidatingly large gun off the man's back and knocking him in the head with the end of it, sending him keeling back into the fourth soldier, who drew his gun, only to have it kicked from his hand, clattering across the deck.

It was her uncle David who ended it, pulling out his own gun and grabbing her by the arm, shoving the cold metal up under her jaw so hard her head snapped sideways.

"Stop!"

The soldier spun around, his blue eyes immediately sizing up the situation. "Let her go."

Lillian glanced at her parents, who were cowering in the doorway of the pilothouse. She waited for them to reprimand her uncle, to demand he put away the gun that he held to her head.

They shrank back, fear on their faces, and said nothing.

"You'll come with me." David glowered at the soldier. "And if you make one false move, Lillian won't be here to save you the next time."

The soldier closed his eyes in submission.

The other uniformed men rose from where they'd fallen, warily grasping the soldier as the helicopter that had been hovering just beyond the boat moved closer. Lillian saw that her parents had lowered the sails to keep the whirling rotors from harming them. They must have welcomed her uncle aboard as she'd been below, bandaging up the soldier's face again, the sounds of the helicopter drowned out by the ambient noise of the ship and the sea.

A ladder dangled from the helicopter, and David nodded toward it. "Climb," he told the soldier.

The man stepped forward, grabbed the rungs, and ascended. One by one, the rest of the soldiers followed him up, disappearing into the shadowy bird that hovered over them in the night sky.

David pulled her toward the ladder.

Finally, her father stepped forward. "You can't take Lillian."

"I don't have any choice." David lowered the gun, but kept it pointed at her. "You saw how he responded when I threatened her. He didn't hesitate. She may be the only effective weapon I have against him."

"You won't hurt her?"

"She'll be fine."

Sandra Bardici peeked her head around her husband's shoulder. "Can she change into dry clothes first? She doesn't even have shoes on."

David Bardici looked up and down her simple outfit of khaki pants and a pale pink T-shirt. "Her clothes will dry soon enough. Can you wear those shoes?" He pointed to her sneakers, which were still on the deck where she'd kicked them off earlier.

While Lily hurried to slip into the shoes, her uncle leaned closer to her father. She had to listen closely to hear him over the roar of the helicopter. "Does she know who he is?"

"*He* doesn't even know who he is. The explosions wiped out his memory."

"Temporarily, I hope." David grimaced. "His memory may be our only link to vital intelligence. We need that information as soon as possible."

Lily listened to their conversation with shock pulsing through her veins. She'd never liked her uncle, but to have him suddenly pull a gun on her—worse yet, to use a threat against her life to control the man who'd rescued her from the sea—

rocked her world far more than the angry waves stirred up by the low-hovering helicopter's rotors.

But her uncle David's behavior fit with his personality, even if it was extreme. And her parents—they'd been acting odd since before the trip to Lydia, and even more so once they'd arrived. Their broken promises compiled a strong case against them. Obviously neither of them was about to challenge David's demands.

No, she couldn't expect either of them to help her any more than they'd spoken up to defend her when uncle David had slammed the gun under her jaw. The only person who'd reacted had been the soldier.

The thought of him sent a trickle of comfort through her. She recalled how gently he'd swept the matted hair from her face as he'd propped her up on the life preserver. He'd not only untangled her leg from the rope, but he'd massaged her tight calf muscle, almost as though he'd known the rope had bit into it, causing it to cramp. And then he'd held her, so firmly and so securely, as he'd pulled her back onto the boat.

She couldn't recall a time when she'd felt so protected.

With the shoes on, she stood, and her mother gave her a cursory hug, as she had so many times when Lily headed back to school for the semester. "Please call and let us know what's happening." She looked at David, not even blinking at the gun he brandished. "I don't suppose you can tell us where you're headed?"

"North Africa. We need to get going or we won't have enough fuel left to make it there." David shoved her toward the ladder.

Lillian looked up at the thunderous bird hovering above them, its dark shape blending with the night sky, making it look infinitely large. She wasn't particularly keen on ladders or heights, especially ladders ascending to nowhere, with gun-bearing soldiers awaiting her on top.

"Climb up." Her uncle's voice grew impatient, the threat of his gun reinforcing each word.

She told herself not to be afraid, not because she felt she could trust her uncle, but because she knew the nameless soldier was up there, and she hoped he could protect her. She grasped the nearest rung and began to climb.

He tried to shift his body into a less-uncomfortable position, but the soldiers had used a thick zip tie to bind his wrists behind his back, so he had only limited use of his arms. Shifting his back against the cool metal wall of the helicopter, he stared at the soldiers who sat on the other side of the luggage netting, guns resting across their laps, pointed at him.

No one moved. The bird hovered, waiting for

the man who'd pulled the gun on Lillian—Lillian's uncle David.

Please keep her safe. He found himself praying, though he hadn't realized he was a man of faith. A movement in the doorway caught his attention, and he turned in time to see Lily's wide-eyed face rise into view, her hands white and trembling as she gripped the doorframe and crawled in.

His heart plummeted. They'd brought her along. She looked terrified. What were they going to do with her?

Her uncle David followed with the gun, the door closed, and the helicopter moved forward through the dark sky.

Lillian turned to face her uncle. "Where should I sit?"

"Here." He spun her around so that her back was to him, grabbed a zip tie from the nearest soldier, and strapped her wrists together before shoving her through the opening in the luggage netting.

She fell forward, tried to catch herself, slammed her shoulder into the sloping back wall, and slid down to the floor beside him, her arms restrained behind her back.

He wished he could reach out to her and help her in her efforts to sit. She rose halfway up, bracing herself against the steep slope of the back wall as though trying to put some distance between them, but there wasn't room in the cramped stowage space.

Lillian slumped down again, her face against his arm. A silent sob shuddered up through her, and she sniffed.

He wanted to comfort her, but he didn't want to get her in more trouble by doing so. The soldiers on the other side of the netting had their guns pointed their way, but other than that, didn't seem to be paying them much attention. Her uncle had disappeared into the seat next to the pilot, and seemed oblivious to his niece or anyone else behind him.

The inside of the helicopter was dark—too dark to make out any details. And the ambient noise of the flying craft drowned out whatever the soldiers were muttering about to each other.

He could only assume it would do the same, masking his words to Lillian. "Are you all right?"

"Fine." Her voice sounded small, and her sniffles reverberated against him. "I'll try to move over, out of your way."

"Don't worry about it. You can lean on me. If you stay close, we can talk without being overheard."

She fell silent. Probably trying to decide if she even wanted to talk to him.

"I'm sorry I got you into this mess. You should have left me in that alley and not looked back."

"Would that have made my uncle less of a horrible man?"

"His horrible actions wouldn't have been directed at you, then."

"Then I would never have known how awful he was. I might have continued thinking of him as a respectable person." She shifted her face around, bracing her cheek against his arm, until her head was tipped up enough that her words were aimed at his ear, and he could hear her clearly, though she kept her voice low. "I would rather know the ugly truth than live in the comfort of a lie."

"You sound as though you've thought this through."

"I've had to do a lot of thinking lately." She stopped fighting her position and left her cheek pressed against his shoulder. "And I think we need to figure out what's going on, and get away from my uncle as soon as we can."

He liked the way she thought. "I agree. Unfortunately, I'm afraid I won't be of much help in sorting out what's going on."

"You don't remember anything?"

"I remember you. You pulled me from the alley, you gave me water when I was thirsty and you bandaged my face after I pulled you from the ocean. That's the total sum of my knowledge at this point."

She sighed.

"Sorry I can't be of any more help than that, but it does make me indebted to you, considering you're the only person I've met this evening who hasn't attacked me."

"Do you know anything about North Africa?"

"Why?"

"That's where we're headed—unless my uncle lied to my parents, which wouldn't surprise me."

"This helicopter can only travel about 500 miles without refueling. Assuming it came from Lydia, the northern coast of Africa would be about as far as it could go in one trip."

Lily sat up a little straighter. "How can you possibly know *that,* and still not know your own name?"

He shrugged. "Ask me another question. Maybe you can trick me into revealing who I am."

She huffed, whether out of frustration or incredulity, he wasn't sure. But she quickly rose to his challenge. "All right. My uncle said that your memory was their only link to vital information that they need right now. Any idea what that means?"

He pinched his eyes shut and tried to think. "I know something they don't?"

"I'd gathered that much from the context. Whatever it is, they seem intent on gleaning that information from you."

"How are they going to do that? Traditional interrogation methods won't work if I can't access my own memory." His heart started thumping ominously. If the men were desperate for information, they'd likely resort to drastic measures, but if he had vital intel they couldn't risk letting him die, so obviously too much torture would be out of the question.

Lillian seemed to realize the answer just as he did. "My uncle said they needed to bring me along because of the way you reacted when they threatened me. He said I was their most valuable weapon against you."

His blood ran cold, and he realized he'd clenched his hands into fists that were useless, bound as he was. Of course. They wouldn't torture *him*— they'd torture *her,* and make him watch until he spilled every secret he had.

Except that he had no way of spilling any secrets, not if he couldn't remember anything. Innocent Lillian would suffer, and there would be nothing he could do about it.

The depth of conviction in his voice surprised him. "We'll have to get away from him quickly. Maybe even as soon as we reach the ground. The faster we can make a break for it, the more likely our plans are to succeed."

"How do you know that?"

"I don't know." He shook his head. "Something

tells me, once we get to wherever we're headed, there won't be any way out."

Lillian panted slightly, clearly wrestling with what he'd told her.

He felt the need to devise a plan. "Do you know anything about North Africa?"

"Not much," she confessed. "Hasn't North Africa been in the news for years now because of violence and fighting and militant groups?"

"You're right. It's a very unstable part of the world, with an inhospitable desert climate." An image shifted through his thoughts, blowing like desert sand, and he felt the sting of it, the oppressive heat, the thirst, the desolation. Like the mirage of a desert oasis, it evaporated as he tried to focus on it, leaving only the lingering image of what once was, or might have been. He grasped at it, but it slipped through his fingers like so much blowing sand.

He opened his eyes to find that Lily had straightened up, pulling her face close to his, watching him.

"Did you remember something?" she whispered as though afraid her words might scare off the wisp of memory.

"I think—" he swallowed, trying to chase the thought, but the sand filled in the footprints more quickly than he could follow them "—I think I've been there before."

"That's good."

"Is it?"

"Maybe you'll know your way around."

"Maybe." He swallowed, his thirst intensified by the mere thought of the desert. He wanted to believe Lillian was right, but from the cold clenching of his gut, he was pretty sure his last visit to the northern coast of Africa hadn't been good at all.

Lily told herself to focus. The mystery of the soldier's identity teased her imagination, pulling her thoughts away from forming a plan. But she didn't have time to waste wondering who the man beside her really was. He'd proven himself to be trustworthy—more trustworthy than her parents, and far more than her uncle. So it didn't matter, then, who he was. He was her only ally, and they needed to work together.

He must have been thinking along the same lines, because he whispered, "It would be helpful if we could get these zip ties off our wrists. We won't get far without the use of our arms."

"You're right. I didn't get a very close look at what they used, but I think they're a basic zip tie like any other, with a ratcheting mechanism that keeps them closed tight. I did an internship at a veterinary clinic and a lot of our supplies came zip tied together. I got pretty good at backing the ratchet out."

"Do you think you could work my hands free?"

"It's worth a try. Can you get your hands where I can reach them? Don't let the soldiers see what we're doing."

Shifting subtly, Lillian managed to get her hands aimed at the soldier, who'd turned his body at a similar angle toward her. She found his fingers, and he gave her hand a reassuring squeeze, distracting her for a moment with the comfort he offered in that tiny gesture. It reminded her that she wasn't alone—that even though they were no longer facing one another, he was with her, working for her freedom as much as his.

She found the nylon strap of the zip tie he'd been bound with, and located the ratcheting mechanism with her fingers. If it was like the ones she'd encountered at the vet clinic, all she had to do was squeeze the head to open up the ratchet box, then depress the engaged ratchet enough to slide it out from the rack. In concept, the steps were easy enough for her to envision.

But with her arm muscles already cramping from their awkward position, and unable to see what she was doing, coaxing the two sides apart proved to be a difficult trick. She squeezed the stubborn plastic box with her fingernails, trying to apply just the right amount of pressure to weaken its hold on the strap.

Finally, it slipped back the slightest bit, and her

heart rejoiced for a moment before the box caught on the very next ratchet.

It would take her all night at this rate!

They didn't have all night. In fact, she suspected they didn't have very long at all. Repeating the motions that had worked before, she tried to ease the strap back another notch, but her hand began to cramp from the constricted angle required to pinch the zip tie.

She flexed her fingers.

"Are you all right?"

"Hand cramp. I just need a second. It's working." When the spasm at the base of her thumb stopped throbbing, she squeezed the zip tie again, trying to direct her motions for maximum effectiveness. The strap popped back one notch, and she flexed her fingers while a bead of sweat trickled down her arm. She pinched again, loosened it another notch and kept going. As she worked, the molded nylon became more pliant, allowing her to slip it past the notches more freely.

"Stop there," the soldier requested when she had the zip tie near the end of its length. "I'll be able to slip my hands out through the loop when I need to, but I want to give the appearance of still being bound. If they realize we're loose, they'll only tie us up again."

Lillian saw the wisdom of his plan. "Do you think you can work me free?"

"I can try. How did you do it?" He leaned closer to her as they spoke, but kept one hand on her fingers.

Lily told herself he was holding on so that he didn't have to find her hand again, but at the same time, the security of his touch calmed her heart. She found her voice, and explained how she'd backed the ratchets out. "Think you can do it?"

"My fingers aren't as nimble as yours, but I don't see any other way of getting you free. Let me have a go at it."

Turning away from her again, he tugged on her arm until he could reach the zip tie, and she felt him struggle to work the tricky notches free.

As he'd hinted, his larger hands weren't as dexterous as her agile fingers, but he kept working on the zip tie, in spite of his lack of progress.

"Do you need to try something else?" she asked after several long, fruitless minutes.

"I think I'm getting closer. It's tricky. Do you have a better idea?"

"Nothing."

"Then I'm going to keep at it. I'm not about to give up." His determination with the obstinate zip tie spoke volumes about his commitment to keeping her with him as he made his escape, which Lillian found reassuring. After all, he was strong and, based on the way he'd overcome the four armed men on her father's boat, obviously a skilled fighter. If either of them had a shot at freedom, he was clearly far better equipped to make his bid. If she got left behind, she'd be at her uncle's mercy.

And she didn't believe for one second the promise he'd made to her parents, that she'd be fine. Uncle David had lied through his teeth. He'd tied her up and shoved her into the stowage compartment as though she was nothing more than a piece of luggage. She was a weapon to him, valuable only as long as she was useful. If the soldier escaped without her, she'd no longer be useful to her uncle. She didn't want to think about what might happen then.

Just as she began to fear her zip tie was a lost cause, she felt its tight hold slacken slightly.

"I'm making progress." Relief filled his voice.

"Good." Lily didn't want to distract him, but the whir of the rotors had lowered in pitch. They were slowing down, likely approaching their destination and preparing to land. They might not have much longer. "If you can get it loose enough, maybe I'll be able to squeeze my hand out."

"Whatever happens, whether I get you free or not, I want you to follow my lead when we disembark."

"What's your plan?"

"It will depend on where we are, how many

men are on the ground and what kind of weapons they're carrying."

The mere thought of armed men sent a shudder rippling through Lily.

He obviously felt it, because he quickly reassured her. "We'll have the element of surprise on our side. They won't be expecting us to make any sort of move. We'll use that to our advantage."

"But we're already outnumbered."

"True. But you said earlier they need the knowledge that's in my head. They're not going to risk killing me."

Lily swallowed. "What about me?"

"I thought that David fellow was your uncle."

"Yes, but you saw how he tied me up and shoved me back here. I don't have any critical information in my head." As she spoke, they shifted with a hollow thump. The helicopter's skids settled to the ground. They'd landed. And though the soldier had worked the zip tie back a few more notches, Lillian was still securely restrained. She wasn't even sure she could stand up without help.

"He's not going to hurt you."

"How do you know that?"

"I won't let him."

FOUR

One of the armed men grabbed Lillian roughly by the shoulder, hauling her to her feet, shoving her in the direction of the door. She couldn't imagine climbing down a ladder with her hands still bound, but as she blinked into the courtyard outside, she saw in the illumination of fluorescent yard lights that a set of wheeled steps had been pushed into place.

Wherever they were, these folks were obviously used to receiving helicopters if they had a set of steps handy.

"Go down," her uncle instructed her from just beyond the armed man's shoulder.

Lily hesitated. She didn't want to go anywhere alone. She and the soldier hadn't had time to discuss any specifics of their plan. He'd said he needed to see what he was dealing with before he would know how to act. Perhaps the best thing she could do was disembark so he could get a good look at what was going on outside.

Her legs, tired from pedaling the rickshaw up and down the hills of Sardis all day, and cramped from the ride in the helicopter, trembled as she tried to descend without the free use of her arms for balance. When she nearly keeled sideways on the second step, the armed man clenched her shoulder with one hand, jerking her backward.

She decided that if it came to a fight, she'd feel no compunction hitting him.

As she made her way down the steps, she looked around, trying to spot some means of escape. High stone walls encircled the enclosure, with a gated door at one end guarded by more armed men, and a fortresslike building along the other side. The heavy wooden doors looked impenetrable. The sound of crashing surf carried through the still night air. They must be near the ocean.

Her damp sneakers squeaked against the cobblestone floor of the courtyard, and she braced herself, ready for the soldier to make his move. She half expected him to leap from the helicopter doorway and take out the soldiers in one mighty pounce, but instead he kept his hands behind his back and his head down submissively.

The armed men shoved them toward the building. Lily went, though inside her heart was screaming. If they entered the building, they might never come out. They needed to do something. They needed to fight!

Two guards held a door open, and Lily stepped through to a marble hallway. She could hear the soldier's footsteps behind her, and she perked up her ears for any change in rhythm that might indicate he was about to make his move.

He plodded on, so she did, too. They passed several closed doors, then changed direction as the hallway bent ninety degrees. If she had her guess, they'd entered the back way and now were headed toward the front of the imposing structure. As she moved, she tugged her arms against the nylon straps that bound her. The soldier *had* managed to loosen the zip ties considerably. In fact, if she thought she could do it without being seen, she just might be able to squeeze her wrists free.

Ahead she saw two multipaned French doors opening to a large, gracious parlor, its high arched windows showcasing only darkness outside. She caught a glimpse of a few twinkling stars, and the longing to be outside distracted her for a moment.

The soldier's sudden movement caught her unaware. If she hadn't heard the grunt of the guard collapsing behind her, she might not have even realized anything was happening. Before she could spin around, the soldier had looped an arm around her waist and swept her into the parlor. He pulled the French doors shut after them, and the velvet door curtains had almost settled into place when they were kicked open again.

"Hold your fire!" David Bardici barked at the guards who'd raised their guns. "Capture them both alive!"

The guards dived forward, but just as quickly the soldier who'd rescued her grabbed a floor lamp that looked to be made of heavy wrought iron and swung it like a bat, sending the first man crumpling down with an ugly welt on his forehead. The next guard ducked, diving for the soldier's legs, but he got knocked on the back of his head and slumped on top of his comrade.

Twisting and squeezing, Lily shifted her hands free of the zip ties. She counted six more men besides her uncle. They split up, clambering over and around the prone figures on the floor, giving the lamp-brandishing soldier wide berth.

With shock, she realized they were coming after *her*. Of course. The soldier had already demonstrated that the easiest way to subdue him was to threaten her.

A second matching floor lamp stood on the other side of a wood-inlaid sofa. She grabbed the lamp, hefting its surprising weight and attempting to brandish it in a threatening manner toward the guards who approached her. The heavy base drooped toward the wood-inlaid parquet floor.

Heaving it upward, she swung it around. Once she got it moving, the momentum carried her in a complete circle.

"Lily!" the soldier shouted. "Facedown on the chaise—now!"

She staggered backward toward where she'd spotted a delicately arched, crème-velvet chaise bench near one of the twelve-foot-high windows. Nearly tripping over the lamp cord, she dropped the heavy thing and dived onto the lightweight chaise, curling into a ball and instinctively covering her head. She didn't know what the soldier was planning, but she wasn't about to get in his way.

The sound of breaking glass nearly drowned out her uncle's words as he screamed, "You can't go through the window! It's a thirty-meter drop with rocks below!"

She thought her uncle David's warning sounded ominous enough, but before he'd hardly finished his sentence, the chaise rocked beneath her as the soldier lifted the dainty bench with her clinging to its sides. She could hear the crash of waves outside and guessed the ocean to be directly below them. The soldier must have heard it, too.

Lily opened one eye in time to see the soldier hoisting the antique piece toward the gaping mouth of the wide-open window he'd broken out. She held on tight to the chaise as he hurled her through to the darkness beyond.

Cool air lifted her hair, blasting her face as she sailed through the darkness into the open sky. Terror struck her. What had the soldier done? She couldn't see anything in the dark night, but she could hear waves crashing below, and smelled the iodine tang of the seashore.

"Hold on!" His voice echoed off the cliffs behind her, and she realized he'd leapt out after her.

She hit the sea with an awful, jarring crack, and her face smashed into the padded arm of the chaise, squashing her nose and sending tears springing to her eyes. The soldier landed behind her on the back of the bench an instant later, sending it lurching backward. "Are you all right?"

"I don't know." She looked around, but could see little in the darkness, save for the closest foam-tipped waves that churned around them, peeling back to reveal menacing rocks like the teeth of a giant, hungry and ready to swallow them.

The soldier had hold of the sides of the chaise, and its lightweight wooden frame proved to be just enough to keep them afloat. As it was, the bench rode low in the water, nearly submerged by the foamy waves. "Keep it balanced. If we tumble off, the undertow could get us."

It was all Lily could do to nod and keep a grip on the upholstery as the salty spray soaked her face, stinging her eyes. "Where do we go from here?"

"I don't know. The waves are pushing us back. Perhaps we can get ashore?"

If he hadn't been behind her, and she hadn't

been clinging for dear life to the sodden couch, she might have tried to shake him. Instead she shook off the waves that had doused her and screamed back, "Next time, you've got to have a better plan than this."

"I got us out of there, didn't I?"

"I'm not sure which is worse." As she spoke, the couch lurched backward on the crest of a particularly swelling wave, shoving the foot of the chaise into the cliff face behind them.

"Here now." The soldier's arms wrapped securely around her, and his voice carried much closer to her ears, deeper now that he wasn't shouting, echoing against the overhanging rocks.

"Where are we?" Her teeth chattered, not so much from the chill of the constant spray, but from fear.

"Hard to say." He rocked as another wave pushed them farther back, then pulled her up a bit more, as though preparing to step off the security of the sofa with her. "It appears the waves have worn out a groove here under the cliff face, like a wide-open cave."

Lily clutched at the upholstery as the soldier tugged her backward. "You're not thinking of leaving the chaise, are you?"

"It snapped in two when we hit the water. The fabric is the only thing holding it together. It won't last much longer." He leaned back toward the solid rock, away from the crashing waves.

She hesitated to follow. "Is it safe?"

"I don't know. But I can guess it won't be long before your uncle sends someone down here to look for us. They can't see us from above because we're under the lip of the rock, but we need to be gone before anyone arrives." As he spoke, he hauled her off the sodden sofa, which was quickly becoming waterlogged and losing all its buoyancy.

The soles of Lily's sneakers crunched against the gravel spit at the base of the cliffs. "So we're going to strike out and pray we don't get smashed against the cliff, or fall into the sea or run out of horizontal ground to walk on?"

He pulled her closer as he leaned back against the cliff side, keeping them away from the bulk of the spray, the crashing fury of the waves muffled by his strong arms. "Have you got a better idea?"

She couldn't think of anything besides the very appealing idea of holding tight to his strong arms, burying her head in his shoulder and pretending there was nothing else in the world beyond the man who held her.

But that wouldn't get them anywhere, except caught again by her uncle. She couldn't let that happen. "Which way do you think we should go?"

He peered into the darkness in either direction. "Most of the North African coast is white sand."

Lily didn't see any white sand, only cliffs and gravel. "Then where are we?"

"If your uncle really brought us to North Africa, then we must be about a hundred kilometers north of Benghazi. That's the only place I know of on the North African coast with cliffs like this."

The thought of plodding a hundred kilometers along the slippery cliff face made her stomach churn. She didn't question how the soldier could recall so many geographic details, but didn't remember anything about himself. Obviously his amnesia had only affected the personal parts of his memory. His intelligence was keen, and highly functional. In fact, his detailed knowledge of the area was slightly unnerving, but she didn't have time to evaluate what it meant. "So we should head south?"

"Southwest." He nodded. "That sounds like the best route. This spit we're walking along should transition to beach within a few kilometers."

Lily kept tight hold of the soldier's right hand with her left as she stepped forward, following him southward. They proceeded in single file along the precarious path as the waves splashed against their feet. The gravel spit beneath grew narrower instead of wider until, as they came to the sharp curve of a promontory, the spit of sand they walked upon disappeared completely.

"Careful now." The soldier peered around the point of the bluff.

Holding tight to the soldier's hand, Lily tried to peek past his wide shoulders, but between the darkness and the spray that splashed freely on the unprotected point, she couldn't make out any sign of further footing.

"Now what?" she asked as he hesitated.

"The sand spit has washed away at the tip of this outcropping, but I'm sure it starts back up again on the other side."

"You're sure?" She didn't think he sounded so sure.

"It should."

"What are you suggesting?"

"You could hold tight to my arm, and I could swing you around to the other side."

"And if there isn't anywhere to stand on that side?"

"I'll pull you back around."

Lily stared at the waves that relentlessly beat against them, dousing them in a constant bath of brine. Her sneakers had long before filled with water, and she was soaked to the skin for the second time that night. She tried to visualize what the soldier suggested. It was as though they walked along a ledge that bent around a corner of a building. He was simply going to hold her steady as she negotiated the curve. The maneuver would have been simple enough, had it not been dark. And wet. And slippery.

And if she knew for certain there was a spit of land to walk upon around the corner.

As though sensing her uncertainty, the soldier offered, "I'd go, but I'm too heavy for you to swing me around. We'd both end up in the ocean."

His words reminded her of the possibility of a strong undertow that might suck them down forever if it got hold of them. "You'll keep tight hold of my hand?"

"Better yet, I'll hold your wrist, and you hold mine." He placed his hand just past hers, and his secure grip enfolded her wrist. "That way, if either of us loses our grip, the other one will still be holding on."

She told herself to relax as she held tight to his arms. He was strong. She could trust him. Couldn't she? "You can't see anything around the corner?"

"It's too dark. Everything is in shadows under the lip of the cliff." He paused. "I don't want to rush you, but your uncle's men could catch up to us at any moment. We need to get moving."

"What if we run right into them?"

"We're south of his stronghold now. They'd be most likely to begin their search there." The soldier peered into the night along the direction they'd come. Suddenly his body tensed.

"What?" Lily turned in the direction he was looking.

Light appeared on level with the sea from beyond where they'd crashed the chaise. Between the spray and the distance, Lillian couldn't be sure, but it looked as though a boat had set out from somewhere to the north.

"Are they looking for us?"

"I doubt it's anyone on a pleasure cruise in the middle of the night. Not with the partially submerged rocks in this area."

"They'll have to stay back from the shore."

"That won't stop them from spotting us."

As he spoke, a distant section of the cliff was illuminated with a bright searchlight, the beam cutting through the darkness, highlighting every jagged crag. It wouldn't be long before the boat crept closer, and the search party shone the light upon them.

"Okay." Lily held tight to the soldier as she scrambled in front of him on the miniscule footpath. "Swing me around."

His strong hand continued to grasp her wrist, and she gripped his arm for all she was worth.

"Ready?"

She nodded, and practically leapt around the corner, scrabbling with her free hand for a hold on the cliff, the soles of her sneakers scraping rock until her right foot slid to a solid spot.

The path! Not only did it reappear on the other side of the promontory, but it widened considerably as it went along.

"It's safe. There's a path," she called out, not daring to raise her voice high enough to be heard by the search party. Fortunately the crashing waves drowned out her words.

"Stay back. I'm coming around."

Lily shuffled back to make room for the soldier. He leapt around, hugging the cliff, and nearly missed the path altogether before Lily reached for him, tugging on his T-shirt to carry him around.

She stumbled backward, trying to haul him onto the spit as he clambered after her. A moment later they each had both feet on the stretch of sand, and she steadied herself against his solid torso as she caught her breath.

"You gave me a scare there."

"There's no time to be frightened. We need to hurry." He held her hand and pulled her along as they darted single file along the sand spit.

The pathway weaved and dipped as it followed the craggy coastline, in some places almost disappearing where the surf had washed away the sand. But the soldier kept tight hold of her hand and fear pushed her to move quickly. After rounding several less-prominent corners, they came to a beach a couple of meters wide tucked under the cliffs, and paused to catch their breath.

"Any sign of the search boat?" she asked, gulping air after their frantic run.

"Not since we rounded that first promontory. I hope they decided to thoroughly search the area around the chaise before proceeding along the coast. That would buy us some time."

"And I hope—" she straightened, finally able to breathe without a stitch pinching her side "—they don't have more than one search boat."

The soldier squeezed her hand as though he agreed with her. "We should keep moving."

She nodded. "After you."

They plodded forward for what felt like miles, though Lily wondered if the darkness only made it seem longer. Her feet squished inside her sodden shoes, so when the beach cut back and the cliffs fell away to a small, rock-strewn canyon, she sat down on a boulder and grabbed a sneaker, intending to pull it off.

"Not here." The soldier tugged her up. "They might yet decide to refuel the helicopter and come looking for us. We'd be easy to spot from the sky."

She stood, but her legs shook from exhaustion. "I'm tired and thirsty, and the skin on my feet is blistering and rubbing off."

Already the blackness of the eastern sky had given way to a gray-green predawn hue, casting just enough illumination for them to see what lay up the canyon. "This way. There's an overhang that should camouflage us from the sky. We can lay low there for a while." He led her inland up the canyon to the spot where an oblong boulder provided enough of a bench for both of them to sit.

Lily all but collapsed onto the rock and tugged at her right shoe, but between the swollen canvas and her slippery-wet hands, she struggled to get it off.

"Allow me." The soldier crouched in front of her and removed both shoes before easing off her sodden socks.

"Thank you." Lily squeezed the excess water from the socks.

"Those will dry quickly once the sun comes out."

"Are we staying put that long?"

"The sun will be rising soon." He looked up and down the canyon before settling down beside her on the boulder and tugging off his boots. "I don't know where we are or where we might find a town around here. Once the sun gets up in the sky, it's going to be too hot to keep going, never mind that we haven't had anything to drink in ten hours."

"So, you're saying we don't have a choice."

He shook his head glumly and pulled off his socks.

"How safe are we here?"

"From our enemies, or from the threats of the North African wilderness?"

"Both."

He shrugged. "Your uncle seemed pretty determined to get his hands on me, and from what I could tell, he has plenty of resources at his disposal. I wouldn't underestimate him. This area looks like the best place to hide. We can take turns resting and keeping watch."

Lily agreed with his assessment. "And the wilderness?"

"We're going to need to find water."

"This canyon looks like it was formed by a stream, but I don't see any sign of water now."

"It's a wadi—a gully that fills with runoff whenever the rains come. But we don't want it to fill with water while we're here. A flash flood could fill this basin, and we'd have no way to escape."

"So, where are we going to find water?"

"I'll come up with something. Why don't you lie down close to the cliff there and rest? You've been up all night and you look beat. I'll keep watch, walk the perimeter, and see if I can't find us some water."

"Rest," Lily repeated. "That sounds fabulous." She rose to her feet and picked her way across the rocky sand toward the deepest part of the shade.

"Lillian?" He ran up behind her, and she felt a

flush of awareness at the sound of the concern in his voice.

"Yes?"

"Be sure to check for snakes and scorpions before you lie down."

"Oh." She nodded sharply, and hoped the darkness was still deep enough to cover the blush that rose to her cheeks. She cleared her throat, erasing any sound of disappointment from her voice. "Snakes and scorpions. Got it."

FIVE

He waited until Lily had settled in to rest before padding barefoot up the wadi. He wouldn't go far. A pale predawn glow already colored the eastern sky, and once the sun hit the sand, the temperature would quickly soar. The scorching sand would burn his bare feet. But he still had time before the sun rose that high, and for now, he'd rather walk barefoot than wear soggy boots any longer.

Though he hadn't wanted to give her cause to worry, the threat of poisonous snakes and scorpions was too great for him to let Lily settle in without checking for the dangerous creatures first, especially with daylight chasing the animals back under cover. Neither of them could afford a venomous encounter at this point. But even an eight-inch scorpion couldn't scare him as much as their far more pressing concern.

They didn't have any water. They wouldn't make it a day without something to drink—preferably three gallons each in this heat, five if they intended to do any walking. They had no way of carrying water with them, and other than the undrinkable seawater that crashed against the shore, they weren't likely to find a reliable source.

But after walking through much of the night, he was willing to settle for any source of drinking water. They'd have to quench their thirst soon, or the desert sun would bake them dry and they wouldn't live to see another evening.

As if to remind him of how quickly the heat was approaching, the sun rose above the horizon, bathing the wadi in its first pink glow. The light might help him find water, but the dangerous summer rays would soon roast the wadi like a stonewalled oven.

He scoured the sand for any sign of animal tracks. This close to the shore the Sahara wasn't such a desolate, sand-washed wasteland. There were scrubby bushes and even a few scattered, spindly trees. Compared to the desert farther south, it was lush. But there still wasn't any sign of drinking water.

Somewhere along the coast there was bound to be a town, however small it might be. But given the size of David Bardici's compound and the forces he employed there, it stood to reason that he would be well-known, and likely influential in the area. No, they couldn't risk visiting a town. Word of their arrival would surely get back to

David quickly, more quickly than they'd be able to rent a car or find a bus. He'd come too far to risk recapture now.

He studied the ground as the sun rose. When he saw tiny paw prints etching the salty surface of the rocky ground, he followed them. A mammal had passed that way, something small, maybe a jerboa or fennec fox—the hard earth didn't permit enough of a print to identify the animal, but its path was still traceable as it scratched its way along the floor of the wadi.

As he'd hoped, other tracks soon crossed the path. Animals had been congregating here. There was water nearby.

But where?

The ground looked dry, but the tracks soon dispersed again. He retraced his steps to the point where the etchings on the ground converged. In the light of the rising sun, shadows colored the ground—the shadows of rocks, of bushes and the occasional low, scrubby tree.

For bushes and trees to grow there had to be an underground water source.

A shadow caught his eye—a dark patch that had no rock or tree to block the sun's light. He grabbed a flat rock and started to dig.

The earth was damp, but shifted freely. He wasn't the first creature to pierce the soil in hopes of quenching his thirst. Like the others, he would cover the spring with sand again to protect its priceless liquid from relentless evaporation.

Finally, as his arms began to ache from digging, he pulled back enough sand to expose a tiny pool of water. Sand swirled where he'd disturbed it, but slowly settled out, leaving a clear pool deep enough for him to dip his hand into it.

Water.

He scratched back enough sand to create a salad bowl-size puddle, then scooped with his cupped palm, drinking mere drops at a time, patiently, until his thirst was quenched. And then, with the sun hauling its unwelcome heat higher into the morning sky, he hurried back to find Lillian.

Though he didn't want to wake her, he had no choice. She'd have to have water before they could strike out again. Their enemies might discover them at any time, and they wouldn't have time for her to quench her thirst if they had to run for their lives.

"Lillian?" He whispered her name, reluctant to disturb her when she looked so peaceful.

Her eyes popped open, but the fear on her startled face receded when she saw him. "Is everything okay?" She sat up slowly.

"I found water."

He didn't have to say anything more. She hopped up and grabbed her socks, which had crusted dry.

His shoes had also dried in the desert heat. He pulled them on, leading her toward the spring, demonstrating how to scoop the water one handful at a time.

"I wish we had a way to carry water with us. I was fortunate to find this spot. Once we leave the wadi, our chances of finding a spring will be even smaller."

Lily looked up from scooping water to her mouth. "When are we leaving the wadi?"

"Not until this evening—unless we're spotted before then."

"Which way will we go?"

"I haven't decided yet. We could head inland, but we can't travel more than one night's walk without a water source. Our other choice is to keep following the coast." He frowned.

"What's wrong with that idea?" She went back to scooping water.

"That's where your uncle David is most likely to be looking for us. And there's hardly any cover along the coastline. We'd be easier to spot and have nowhere to hide."

Lillian drank quietly for several more minutes, scooping the water by patient handfuls to her lips. Finally she sat back and regarded him. "I think we should rest near this spring today. When the sun starts to go down, we can drink as much as we can hold, and then start up the wadi. If we haven't found a road or town or another water source by morning, we can always come back here. We're not in any hurry, are we?"

"Other than escaping from your uncle, I've got nowhere I know of that I need to be." He smiled, knowing there was a good chance that, whoever he was, someone expected him somewhere. But until his memory returned, he didn't know where that might be. "What about you?"

"I was on the run before my uncle entered the picture." She moved back from the spring.

"What were you running from?"

"Reality."

He paused middrink and looked up at her, trying to gauge how serious she was. Her expression was drawn, and he considered for the first time that the fear behind her eyes might have its roots before he'd entered the picture. Full of water, he began to cover the spring with clean sand. "Which reality is that?"

"I'm still trying to sort it out." She shuffled farther back as he scraped the sand over the spring with the flat digging rock.

Finally, satisfied that their water source was amply protected, he shuffled over and joined her in the shade of a few scrubby trees that marked the location of the spring. Since she hadn't spoken again, he offered, "You don't have to tell me about it unless you want to." But at the same time, he couldn't help but be curious.

"Thanks for understanding," she said quietly. After a moment, she stood. "Why don't you rest now? I can keep watch."

"Do you know what you're watching for?"

"Bad guys? Scorpions and snakes?"

He stretched out in the shade. "Keep an eye out for any sign of civilization or water."

"I'll do that."

Lillian slowly expanded her circle as she wandered from one shady spot to the next, exploring the area surrounding where the soldier rested near the spring. He'd warned her that the real desert began in earnest farther south, but she still thought their surroundings were plenty desolate, a never-ending stretch of rocky sand pockmarked by stiff bushes and patches of brittle grass.

Hoping to find some sign of the civilization or water she'd been told to look for, Lily made her way up the side of the ravine to the plateau above. From there, she could see far out to sea, but there were no boats in the area. She squinted northward, expecting to spot some sign of her uncle's fortress, but the craggy bluffs mounted higher in the distance, blocking any sign of the stronghold from which they'd escaped in the night. They'd traveled farther than she'd realized.

To the southwest, the rocky promontory tapered

off, and in the distance the sea met the shore with wide sandy beaches gleaming white in the sun. She turned her gaze farther south—inland, where the Sahara seemed to stretch on forever.

Heat simmered up from the desert in waves, distorting the sand and sky into a blur that stung her eyes. And yet, as she strained to see, a dull cloud rolled across the southern horizon, churning up the sand in dusty billows.

Was someone traveling across the distant desert? Where were they headed? Was it her uncle, searching for her?

She watched as the cloud billowed on toward the east. Recalling what little she knew of North African geography, she figured herself to be somewhere west of Egypt.

Did the cloud of sand mark the progress of a caravan headed toward Egypt? If they could reach the travelers beyond them, would they be able to find help and supplies? Lily thought of the wad of bills the soldier carried in his pocket. Assuming he hadn't lost them during their adventures the night before, would they be able to buy water with the money he carried? Lily wished she'd had a chance to grab her purse before leaving the boat, but her uncle had barely allowed her to put on her shoes. She'd have to depend on the soldier's generosity, and promise to pay him back if they ever reached safety.

The thought prodded her conscience. Would she have any way to pay the soldier back? It occurred to her that, before she asked him to do anything more for her, she ought to confess just how desperately poor she currently was. Her life had been through one tumultuous upheaval after another for the past several weeks.

The rising sun seared her uncovered head, its relentless heat a reminder of the danger of the desert. Lily watched the distant dust cloud fade, and realized there was no point waking the soldier to have him look at it. They wouldn't get anywhere until nightfall. And even then, without a source of water, she wasn't sure they could reach the spot where the dust cloud traveled—even if it didn't move far beyond them by the time they reached the place where it now passed.

Clambering back down the side of the canyon, Lily found the shade near the spring where the soldier rested, and lowered herself down to the relative cool in the shadow of a scraggly clump of trees. The soldier lay on his back, the injured side of his face toward her, uncovered since he'd removed the sodden bandages. At least his injuries appeared to be healing, disinfected by their saline bath the night before.

Uncomfortable at the idea of watching him while he slept, Lily closed her eyes, still pondering who the mysterious man might be. He was certainly handsome, and the uninjured side of his face looked almost familiar, though she couldn't begin to place where she might have seen him. During her week in Lydia, she'd seen many soldiers. Perhaps they'd crossed paths then.

The biggest clue to the mysterious man's identity, besides the uniform he'd worn and the money in his pocket, was her uncle's determination to capture and interrogate the man. David Bardici had gone to great lengths to get his hands on this soldier. But why? What knowledge did he have that her uncle was so desperate to get?

The distant rumble of a motor nudged him from sleep. He could tell from the smell of baking sand that he was still in North Africa. But wasn't he supposed to have left? Yes, he was supposed to go home. But why? An event. He'd be getting his next assignment. It was important that he be there.

But who was he?

He sat up and looked around, and immediately recalled all that had happened as far back as the thick blanket that covered his memory. That's right. He was on the run from General David Bardici of the Lydian Army.

And what was that distant rumbling that had awakened him? It sounded as though it came from the direction of the sea, just out of sight around the crags of the canyon.

He glanced around. Lily had said she was going to keep watch, but he spotted her leaning against a tree, her eyes closed. From the angle of her lolling head, he guessed she was asleep.

The sight made him smile. Poor thing was tuckered out. For a moment, he reflected on the mystery of the woman who'd endangered herself to care for him. Why had she done that? He was grateful for her help, but at the same time, he wondered at the events that had taken place on the Bardicis' yacht before his arrival. There was more to the lovely woman than she'd told him. He wanted to learn all he could about her. But now was not the time.

He had to find the source of the rumbling, which grew louder, as though approaching their bivouac. Jumping up, he kept close to the wall of the canyon, poking one eye around the crag to spot the sea.

There. A boat moved past slowly, the men onboard scouring the shoreline, wary of the rocks, but equally intent on their search. Though he didn't see David Bardici among them, these were likely his men. They carried the same weapons as the men the night before.

So they hadn't given up their search. Having seen all he cared to, he ducked back toward their hiding place under the lip of the cliffs. Unless the men on the boat decided to beach their craft and search the wadi, he and Lillian would be safe where they were.

"What's that rumbling sound?" Lily's voice met him as he settled back into the spot where he'd been resting.

She was only a couple of meters away. If they whispered, there was little chance the searching men would hear them, especially not over the sound of the boat. Still, he didn't want to take any chances, but motioned for her to move closer to him.

Lily darted over and took a seat in the shade next to him. "Is it my uncle?"

"I think it might be his men. They're searching the shoreline. So far they haven't ventured inland."

"Do you think they'll see our footprints?"

"The waves should have washed away those that are visible from sea."

Regret chased across her features as she shook her head. "I shouldn't have fallen asleep."

"Would you have been able to prevent the boat from approaching, then?" He shook his head to answer his own question. "You needed your rest. We'll both have to conserve our energy as best we can until we find food."

Lily's face brightened. "I saw a dust cloud earlier, moving far to the south of us. Do you think there might be a caravan traveling through the desert?"

"Could be. The shifting sand makes regular road maintenance almost impossible, so traditional caravans still cross the desert by camel. But bandits roam these deserts, as well as militant rebel groups. By the time we could get close enough to see who they are, they'll have spotted us. Approaching them would be a risky venture, especially since it seems your uncle is powerful in this area. Anyone we encounter could betray us to him."

Rather than be discouraged by his words, Lily's face lit up, and she gripped his arm. "Wait—I just remembered something. The Rising Sun Horse Race is supposed to be traveling through the Sahara, from Tripoli toward Cairo."

"I don't know anything about that," he confessed.

Lily's enthusiasm wasn't diminished. "I've followed it in the news since I was a girl. It's only held every three years. My parents promised me that if I came on this trip with them, we could go to Tripoli in time to watch the race start. But when the time came, they decided to stay in Sardis instead."

Disappointment welled up in her voice as she spoke, and he couldn't help but wonder why her parents had broken their promise, especially when the race happened so rarely, and seeing it clearly meant a great deal to her. "If we could reach the race route, we might be able to blend in. But that doesn't solve our question of food and water." His words dropped off, and Lily's hand clenched around his arm, her eyes wide.

The receding rumble of the boat motor had stopped.

"What do you suppose—" she began in a whisper.

"They've beached it. They're coming inland to search. From the sound of it, they've moved south of us. If they head this way, they'll most likely come up over that ridge, there." He pointed to the opposite wall of the canyon.

"And they'll have a wide-open view of us." Lily looked around frantically. "We've got to find somewhere else to hide."

Having already scoped out the area, he didn't know what to tell her. There was nothing but the canyon and the scraggly bushes, which wouldn't camouflage anything larger than a jerboa.

"The other side of the gully. There's enough of an overhang, if they look down from above they won't be able to see us there."

"Assuming they don't come up the wadi." He peered up and down the ravine. There wasn't anywhere else to hide. "Come on, then. We'll have to erase our footprints as we go. If they spot those it will lead them straight to us."

He snapped off two branches from the nearest

scrubby tree, handed one to her, and demonstrated how to walk backward, wiping away their footprints behind them as they went. Quickly, they shuffled over to the far side of the gully, checked for snakes and scorpions, and ducked under the lip of the rock. There wasn't as much shade on that side, but the dry heat baked all the sweat from their skin.

Muted voices carried through the still air, muffled by the sounds of the seashore beyond them. Lily had hold of his arm again, and he could feel her tension as she strained to hear, listening for any sign that they were about to be discovered.

He brushed the hair back from her ear and pressed his mouth close, whispering, "The safest place for us is right here. Don't panic and try to run away. We'll only run if we're sure they've spotted us."

She nodded. "How many men do they have?"

"I counted eight on the boat."

Lily let out a slow breath.

They were outnumbered. They couldn't risk letting it come to a fight—though he'd managed to fend off that many men and more the night before, he wasn't sure what he was capable of, or why he knew so much about hand-to-hand combat. It wouldn't be wise to depend on his untested skills in defense, not given the odds against them.

A voice carried clearly through the simmering

air. "Let's check the ravine. If they came this way, there's nowhere else they could be."

Lily's lips drew level with his ear. "We need to pray."

He took her hand and squeezed it.

"Lord, please don't let them find us," she began in a whisper.

He let out a silent breath, shushing her, and her words fell away, the soft pulse of her breath against his neck evidence that she continued to pray, murmuring silently as she gripped the hand with which he'd enfolded hers. He pinched his eyes shut and joined her in silent prayer.

The soldiers' voices carried closer. "Let's hurry. I don't like being out in this heat."

"This heat has nothing on the heat Bardici will lay on us if we come back empty-handed."

"He can't expect us to conjure them out of thin air."

"I still say they drowned when they hit the rocks."

"You convince Bardici of that, then."

"He won't believe it unless you find the bodies."

The soldiers' words grew louder, clearer, as the men drew nearer.

"You suppose they're down there?" The voice seemed to come from almost on top of them.

"If they are, you'd think we could see them. There's nowhere to hide."

"Besides that, it's a wadi. Alec knows better

than to hang out there. If a flash flood comes up, he'd be done for."

The name they spoke lodged in his mind. Alec. Was that the name of the man they were looking for? Was that *his* name? It carried through the distant recesses of his mind, spoken by his mother's voice, calling to him. But he didn't have time to answer. He had to pay attention to what the men above him were saying.

"Doesn't look like any flash floods have come through in a while."

"No, but something's been through there. The sand looks disturbed."

Silence. In the tense, empty air, he could almost hear the soldiers adjusting their binoculars.

"Snakes."

"What?"

"See the way the sand shifts in narrow trails? That wadi's full of snakes."

"Poisonous?"

"Most likely."

Sand rained down over the lip of the ravine, sprinkling to the ground just off to his left, as though the men had ventured near the edge, dislodging it.

"Bardici said to leave no stone unturned. We should check down there, just to be sure."

"It's your funeral." More sand pattered down. The men who'd been crouching stood. Metallic clinks and splashing told him they'd pulled out their canteens for a drink.

Suddenly an object cut through the open air in front of him, half burying itself in the soft sand as it landed.

A canteen.

"Titus," a voice scoffed, "you need to be more careful. Are you going down for that?"

Lily's hand gripped his arm tighter. If the men came after their canteen, they'd find them for sure, sitting as they were less than three meters from it.

And every soldier knew better than to let himself become separated from his water in the desert.

SIX

"Forget it. There's no easy way down, and I'm not tangling with snakes over a stupid canteen. Let's get back to base and tell Bardici they're gone."

"He's not going to like it."

"He doesn't like a lot of things."

The men grumbled, but their voices were quickly swallowed up by the distance, and Lily's grip relaxed on his arm.

His gaze didn't leave the canteen. It was a blanket-covered, military-issue four-quart desert canteen with nylon strap, the screw-on lid attached with a chain so it couldn't be lost.

The nylon strap had been extended to accommodate enough play to allow a soldier to drink without unstrapping it from his body—precisely so that it wouldn't be dropped, or lost, or left behind.

He stared at it a little longer. Why had it fallen? Had Titus dropped it on purpose? Did the soldier—it was the same voice that had declared their sweeping brush marks snake trails—really believe the wadi to be filled with poisonous reptiles?

Was Titus baiting him by dropping the canteen? Or had he left his water behind to help them? Why would he try to help them?

Lily inched closer until her mouth was close to his ear. "Should we take the canteen?"

He shrugged, still undecided, and pinched his eyes shut as a name echoed through his thoughts.

Alec! Alec!

His mother was calling him again, wanting him to wake up, to get going.

But who was his mother? And who was he?

The throttle of a distant motor chugged to life. "They're back in the boat. Let's give them time to clear the mouth of the wadi. We don't want to risk them seeing us."

"And then?"

"When we're sure the coast is clear, we'll open up the spring again, drink as much as we can hold, fill the canteen, and head for the dust cloud you saw to the southeast."

"But it's not evening yet."

"I know." He replayed the men's words. Bardici didn't want to leave any stone unturned. If any of the soldiers revealed that the team hadn't searched he wadi, the general might dispatch another team. A larger team, one free of sympathizers—if, indeed, it had been a sympathizer who'd knowingly helped them out by dropping the canteen. "We don't have the luxury of waiting any longer."

Lily drank as much water as she could hold, until her stomach sloshed with her every movement. Then, when the soldier was done drinking his fill, she drank a little more. They made sure the canteen was full before starting off.

Though plenty of daylight remained, the late-afternoon sun was already at enough of an angle to the earth that the sky filtered its light, reducing its burning impact. Still, they kept as much as possible to the ribbon of shade that rimmed the western side of the canyon. Without proper desert clothing, lacking even hats, she knew they were particularly susceptible to sunburn. And they'd have to ration their water carefully.

They started off in silence, still stifled by the threat of the soldiers' possible return, their ears pricked to pick up the rumble of a boat motor or the thump of a helicopter's blades. But they heard nothing more than the tiny whisper of the wind. Even the sounds of the sea faded behind them.

Lily's thoughts churned. She could feel a nasty bruise under her jaw where her uncle had shoved his gun. His betrayal stabbed at her more sharply than the jab of the barrel. And worse yet had been her parents' obsequiousness in the face of David's cruelty. They'd broken promises of late, but this was a new low.

Rather than dwell on the hurt of their actions, she turned her thoughts to the mystery of the man who marched beside her. Who was he? And why was her uncle so determined to capture him?

When they'd traveled far beyond the sound of the sea, Lily asked, "Who's Alec?"

"The name the soldier mentioned back there?"

"Yes. Is that you?"

"Might be."

"It doesn't ring any bells?"

"Not much does."

"But you know about surviving in a desert. You know how to fight. Where do you think you got those skills?"

"When you found me I was wearing a uniform, so maybe I'm a soldier. Maybe I was deployed out here until I got called back to Lydia."

She swallowed, her throat already dry. "Why do you think they called you back to Lydia?"

"There are two possibilities I can think of. One, I was part of something, maybe part of whatever that ambush was trying to attack. Your uncle said I have intelligence they need, right? So either they were attacking to get their hands on me and find out what I know, or else..." he let his voice fade, but kept walking.

She plodded through the desert beside him,

waiting for him to finish his thought. "Or else?" she prompted finally.

"It's possible I'm part of the rebel group that ambushed the motorcade. Maybe I know something about the operation, or maybe I was sent in to learn something."

"You don't sound as though you approve of that possibility."

"I don't approve of your uncle or the way he does business. Granted, I have no memory of anything, so I can't be the best judge, but any man who shoves a gun at an innocent woman..." He shook his head. "Not to mention, I seem to recall that Lydia is a Christian nation. The royal family members are all godly people. I can't condone an attack on them."

Lily's heart beat harder at his zealous proclamation. "I think, if you feel that strongly about it, that should tell you something about who you are."

He paused and looked at her for the first time in their conversation.

Hope rose inside her as she met his eyes. "I don't know who you are, but I know that I trust you—right now, I trust you more than I trust my own parents. You've proven yourself to be worthy of that trust, and they haven't."

He cupped his hand above her forehead, blocking the sun that shone in her eyes as she looked up at him. She stopped squinting and smiled. "Whoever you are, you're a kind, compassionate man. Your actions reveal that."

But his hardened expression didn't soften. "You need to be careful. Until I know who I am, you can't trust me. Not completely." He turned back toward the southeast and pressed on.

Lily followed, the soldier's words a reminder she didn't want to accept. It was almost as though he was telling her to guard her heart against him, but already she cared for him. "Alec?"

"Hmm?" He looked back at her.

She grinned. "You answered to it. I think it *is* your name."

"Call me whatever you like." He kept moving doggedly forward.

They continued in silence, but Lily found she was tired of hearing nothing but their muffled footsteps and the lonely whispers of the wind. Replaying the events of the day before, she tried to sort out what she could of the ambush on the motorcade. Everything had happened so quickly, the blasts erupting from nowhere in the midst of a peaceful, music-filled procession.

The Lydian national anthem had been broadcast from somewhere, and now it stuck in her head, playing in a constant loop as she recalled the words she'd been taught as a child. Finally, unable to stand the silence any longer, she decided to sing. *"O, Lydia, my motherland,"* she began, working her way through the verses, faltering only slightly when her parched mouth struggled to carry the words. But conviction strengthened her voice as she sang the lines, *"None can triumph o'er your walls, where duty, faith and freedom calls."* The ancient words quickened her breath, and her song faded to a whisper as she reached the last line, *"O, Lydia, forevermore."*

As she sang, her steps fell into rhythm with the haunting melody, and she found her feet less inclined to drag. Too soon, the song came to an end, and she caught her breath, swallowing past the dryness of the desert air, preparing to launch into the song again.

But before she found her voice, the soldier next to her picked up the tune, his deep voice a solemn bass as he chanted in the minor key. His masculine intonations caught her so off guard, it took her a moment to realize he wasn't singing in English.

The exotic words that slipped from his lips fit the tune even better than those she'd sung, and her heart beat faster as she hurried to keep up with him, straining to hear each word, though she didn't know what any of them meant. The wadi through which they'd traveled had given way to endless white sand, and the sun sank lower in the sky, stretching their shadows long across the wind-rippled desert floor. They plodded on as he sang, his voice deep, sturdy, strong. She wished he'd keep singing forever, a marching tune for their unending trek.

When he finished the song, the last note lingered in the still air.

"What was that?" she asked once she got up the courage to break the sacred silence.

"The Lydian national anthem."

"In what language?"

"Old Lydian."

A cold shiver chased across her skin in spite of the heat of the desert. No one had spoken Old Lydian in generations—English had been made the official language of the tiny country around the time of the First World War, and everyone had stopped speaking Old Lydian. How did the soldier know it?

"The song was originally written in Old Lydian," she surmised.

"It was composed in the ninth century by Queen Gisela. She was a daughter of Charlemagne, the Holy Roman Emperor."

Lily didn't question how he was able to recall the ancient facts. She'd already determined that only his personal memory had been erased. But she wondered if, perhaps, by tapping into the facts he recalled, she could somehow get him to reveal something about himself that would help them identify who he was. When he fell silent, she prompted him. "Queen Gisela? That's a lovely name."

"I understand she was a lovely woman. Her husband was King John, and her son was King Thaddeus. My brother is named after him."

The revelation caused Lily to stumble, and when the soldier caught her by her arm, preventing her from falling, she looked into his eyes, and could see the window to the past shutter as quickly as it had opened.

Desperate to reach him before the window closed completely, she scrambled to think of something to ask. "You have a brother?" she asked at last.

He blinked, and she could see that the window had closed.

But this time he'd left enough of a trail she hoped they might be able to follow it. "You have a brother named Thaddeus."

"Do I?" He appeared to be genuinely uncertain.

"He was named after King Thaddeus." They'd stopped walking, and Lily had no intention of traveling on, not until she'd plumbed the tiny spring of information to its depths. A thought struck her, and she gripped his forearms with both hands.

"Thaddeus," she repeated. "Is it a common name in Lydia?"

The hollow void behind his eyes held no answers.

She wished she could call back the man who'd peeked out from his walled-off consciousness only moments before. *"Alec."* She repeated the name the soldier had used. "Alexander."

He blinked.

"I went to watch the royal motorcade, to watch the royal family of Lydia pass by. Do you know the names of the royal family of Lydia?"

"King Philip and Queen Elaine."

"Who are they?" She wanted to shake him but resisted the impulse. Instead, she prayed silently that her words would pierce the dark shroud that hid him from himself.

"The king and queen of Lydia."

As an American, Lily had limited knowledge of the Lydian royal family, but her father held joint Lydian citizenship, and her uncle's position high in the military meant that Lydian politics were occasionally discussed in her home growing up—not that she'd ever cared about them enough to listen before. In fact, she'd tended to tune out anything her uncle talked about, simply because she couldn't stand the man.

"Do they have any children?" She moistened her dry lips with her tongue.

"I don't know."

"You've known everything else. You knew about the helicopter's fuel capacity, you knew where to find water in the desert. You know Old Lydian, but you can't remember anything about *yourself.*"

His forehead furrowed, and sorrow etched through the scabs on the left side of his face.

Lily shuffled to his right, staring at his profile. She hadn't seen a picture of the whole royal family of Lydia since the princes were much younger, and yet, it fit. His face fit, the names…everything fit. Her breathing increased as she realized who he might possibly be.

"You can remember facts," she prompted him, "but not personal details. So why can't you recall the names of the princes and princesses of Lydia?"

He stumbled back. He wanted to lie down, but he knew the sand was still baking hot. That simple fragment of knowledge only compounded the truth of what Lillian had said. He knew all about the desert.

He shuddered as ripples of memories tore through him with the force of the searing blasts that had rocked the streets of Sardis.

In spite of his best efforts to stay on his feet, he found himself knocked to his knees by the concussive force, gripping his head, fighting against the flashes that shot through his skull, the brilliant glare of the grenades shrieking through his thoughts.

Rocking forward, he caught himself with his hands, and flinched back as the hot sun scorched his palms.

"You're all right," Lily soothed him, her voice echoing from far away, though he knew she stood right beside him. She held his shoulders and pulled him back, her small hands tugging him from the brink of panic.

He swallowed back his nausea and tried to get a handle on what was happening.

The burning, searing scent of the explosions assaulted him, and the tinny sound of the Lydian national anthem tinkled like a tightly wound music box between his ears.

The princesses—his younger sisters! He had to reach them! They didn't know anything about surviving an ambush. He had to find them.

A blast rocked his body and he grasped the air in front of him, expecting to encounter limestone walls.

There was nothing but arid desert air.

Throwing his head back, he let loose an anguished scream with all that was in him, but still the sound was not loud enough to drown out the terror of the attacks that echoed through his mind.

He screamed again and staggered to his feet. He had to reach his sisters. He had to save them! He stumbled forward.

"Alec?" Lily's voice was patient as she ran along beside him, sprinting to keep up. "Alexander?"

He stopped and shook his head. "I am, aren't I?"

She nodded.

"They're gone?"

"Who?"

"My sisters, my parents—ough!" He cried out again. "My brother, Thaddeus, has been missing for six years." He shook his head, shook his whole body, as though if he could rattle his jumbled brain enough, all the missing pieces might fall back into place. His jaw clenched as the memories surfaced. "General Bardici wants to know where he is."

He flinched as though he'd been struck, then fell to his feet again, the sharp pain against his back nearly enough to make him pass out.

Yes.

He *had* passed out, had awakened in a blur on an airplane bound for home. The needles had pierced his arms with a drug-induced promise. *You won't remember. You were never tortured. You were never struck. The scars on your back are from a childhood tangle with a house cat.* He peeled back the whitewashed words, revealing the lies for what they really were.

He looked up at Lillian, who stood over him with concern knitting her brow.

"Could you look at my back? Are there scars there?"

She didn't move. "Not scars. Scabs. They'll scab over eventually, but they're still fresh. I saw them when we were on the boat."

"How old would you judge them to be?"

"Less than two weeks, maybe even less than one week old. Do you recall how you got them?"

"Could they have been caused by a house cat?"

Lily shook her head and extended her bare arms toward him. "I've made it a habit of trying to rescue every stray that's ever crossed my path." A filigree of white lines etched through her tanned skin like the gossamer threads of a spider's web. "That was no house cat that sliced your back, not even a wildcat or lion. You look as though you were beaten."

"Whipped?"

"Quite likely." Pain knit her features. "Do you remember now what happened?"

He eased himself to his feet, the memories settling into place, though he didn't like any of them. They were ugly, evil things, and if he'd had any choice in the matter, he might have opted to suppress them again. But he needed that knowledge, needed it desperately if he was going to have any chance righting the wrongs against his family. "More than I'd like to."

Alexander plodded forward, a thousand times more determined to get out of the desert. He had somewhere he needed to be. In fact, he was long overdue. "What do you suppose the penalty is for whipping the heir to the throne of Lydia?"

* * *

Lily hurried to keep up with the soldier's angry strides, trying to make sense of the scattered memories he'd flung at her. "Is that who you are, then?"

"I was, before my family was attacked. We've got to get back there. We've wasted so much time."

"Do you think they've unseated your family? How do you know all of this, all of a sudden?" Her heart pounded inside her, a thousand questions raining down through the desert air. Was he really a prince? He'd been whipped? And what *had* become of his family?

Alec met her questions with a question. "What day is today?"

"It's Saturday evening."

"The ambush on the motorcade was just last night—Friday night?"

"Yes."

"Maybe there's still time," he muttered, then took a deep breath and explained. "Eight days ago, your uncle, General David Bardici, called me into his office in Benghazi. I've been deployed there with my unit on a humanitarian mission. I thought he wanted to check on the progress of our work, but he immediately started asking me questions about my brother's disappearance."

"Your brother, Thaddeus?" Lily tried to keep up, not only with the soldier's furious progress across the sand, but the suddenly complex story that had unraveled all around them. In the midst of her struggle to put the pieces together, her heart shouted loudly, *he's a prince! He's a prince!*

"Yes. He's the oldest, the only heir to the throne in line ahead of me. Six years ago, he and his best friend, Kirk, went sailing. Kirk returned alone. No one has heard from my brother since then."

Lily panted as she jogged along. She'd caught some of that story on the national news. "Kirk— he was accused of murdering your brother, wasn't he?"

"Yes, but there was no body. No evidence my brother was actually dead." Alec paused, and for the first time seemed to realize how much Lily was panting. He pulled the canteen off his shoulder and handed it to her. "You look like you could use a drink."

"Thank you." She tipped the bottle back and forced herself to sip slowly of the precious liquid, even while she came to grips with what Alec told her. He was a prince. Her heart burned with the realization, and she realized she had gotten far closer to him than she likely should have. He was far out of her league.

Alec continued his explanation. "Kirk was my friend, too. He wouldn't hurt my brother, and if by accident he did, he would have apologized and explained what had happened. Instead he refused to say what had become of my brother. It made my father absolutely furious. He hasn't been the same since."

Lily handed the canteen back, and waited while Alec took a sip. "Do you know what happened to Thaddeus?"

"No."

"Why would my uncle think you do? And why, if he thought you knew something, would he wait six years to question you?"

"He didn't just question me. He tortured me, trying to get the information he wanted."

"But how could he possibly get away with that? That's got to be highly illegal."

Alec's expression clouded, and he looked down at his arm.

Lily noticed a faint, faded-yellow bruise inside his elbow.

"He gave me something to make me forget. A drug of some sort."

"A memory-erasing drug?"

Alec looked uncertain, and offered her the canteen again. "Is there such a thing?"

"Nothing legal." Lily shook her head, thinking back in time to research rabbit trails she'd followed in her undergrad studies. "There are drugs that are known to have the effect of erasing short-term memories, but they've never been thoroughly researched because their use raises tremendous ethical questions. You can't mess with people's memories. Who would do such a thing?"

Alec met her eyes. "Your uncle?"

His words hit her like a slap to the face. Of course. Her evil uncle, who'd had the prince tortured, who'd put a gun to her head. "I wonder if the effects of the drugs contributed to your amnesia after the attack?"

"I don't doubt they did. But now that my memory is back, I seem to have tapped into those memories, as well." Alec screwed the lid back into place on the canteen and nodded in the direction of their march. As they headed off again, he explained his theory. "That uncle of yours is up to something—something huge. This ambush on the motorcade, torturing and questioning me, it's all been festering for some time, and now it's coming to a head."

She could feel his impatience that he wasn't in Sardis to squash whatever it was that was rising. "What are we going to do? We're hundreds of miles from Lydia, and my uncle's men have been searching for us. If they come back to the wadi and find the canteen missing, they'll know we weren't killed by the rocks or the undertow. Our footprints will lead them straight to us. We can't risk going back the way we came."

"We can't risk doing *anything* that might get us caught again," Alec agreed. "That should be our first priority. I want to find out what's happening back home, as well. Who knows what might have become of my parents and sisters? I can only pray God has kept them safe." He looked up to the sky, where sickly green twilight crept across the desert from the east, as the sun puddled in a pool of red on the opposite horizon.

"And then," he panted, "*somehow,* we've got to get back to Sardis."

Lily shuddered at the thought. "But, Alec? The last time you were there, you were ambushed. They tried to kill you."

"It doesn't matter."

"Why not?"

"Until your uncle and his coconspirators are brought to justice, things are only going to get worse." He continued his march southeast.

Lily had no choice but to follow, though her breath caught as his ominous words clenched like fingers around her heart. Their situation was already dire enough. She couldn't imagine it possibly getting any worse.

SEVEN

Lillian wanted to give the prince all the time he needed to sort out his recovered memories. She was having enough difficulty absorbing the reality that he was a prince. Surely the news was even more shocking to him. But much as she wanted to let him have all the time and space he needed to sort through his thoughts, nonetheless, there were certain tactical details she needed him to stay on top of.

"You realize Sardis is north of here, don't you?" She didn't want to come right out and say it, but they were headed in almost the opposite direction.

"Yes, and what's in between us? Your uncle's compound and the Mediterranean Sea. It's over eight hundred kilometers from Benghazi to Sardis. Traveling by ship, even if we average seven knots, it would take almost three days to get there."

"So, if my parents have been in contact with my uncle, they should be headed toward the coast in hopes of reuniting with me, but they won't make port until late Monday."

"Do you want to be reunited with your parents?" Alec asked with caution in his voice.

Lily considered the question. "My father obviously called David to the yacht. My parents stood by and did nothing while my uncle put his gun to my throat." She shook her head. "I can't imagine trusting them again, and yet, who else do I have?"

"You're an only child?" Alec asked.

"Yes. I have friends back in the United States, but what use is that to us now? Besides—" she cringed as she admitted the truth "—I don't have anyone who cares about me enough to help me out of this mess. My parents always discouraged me from forming close friendships. I'm not particularly close to anyone."

To her mortification, Alec stopped walking and looked at her.

She couldn't meet his eyes, but stared at the sand by her feet.

"That sounds lonely."

The pity in his voice made her wince, though she was certain he was only trying to be kind.

Sympathy filled his words. "Is that why you were so keen on rescuing strays?"

Mustering the courage to look him in the face, she admitted, "I always thought I wanted to help animals for *their* sake. But when my father's horses died...."

Alec bent closer.

She shook her head. The wounds were still too fresh to think about, let alone discuss. "We should get going."

To her relief, Alec didn't push the subject, but pressed onward beside her. "You raise an excellent question, though. We need to figure out how to get to Sardis as quickly as possible."

"Neither of us has a passport with us," she reminded him. "I doubt we could cross the border into Egypt, let alone get on a plane to Lydia."

"A plane would be the fastest way," Alec agreed, "but you're exactly right about our odds of catching one. We lack both the paperwork and the funds."

"Funds!" She grabbed his arm in her excitement, but quickly remembered that he wasn't just a soldier. He was a prince. She didn't have a right to cling to him anymore. She dropped his arm. "You had cash in your pocket. Is it still there?"

Alec fished around in both pockets and pulled out the money clip, complete with a fat wad of bills.

"That is *real* money, I hope."

"African dinar." He spread out the bills. "Several kilo—the equivalent of a few thousand dollars."

"Do you always carry so much money?" The

moment she asked the question, she feared she'd overstepped her bounds, and backpedaled. "You don't have to answer. You're a prince, you can carry whatever you want. It's none of my business." Embarrassed, she decided to keep walking.

Alec refolded the notes and tucked them back into his pocket. He hurried after her. "I don't usually carry this much, but I recently cashed my last paycheck. Anyway, it *is* your business to know. Last I checked we were in this together. You rescued me from the ambush when I didn't even know my own name."

"And then I got you recaptured again."

"How many times did you bandage my face?"

"Only to let it get soaked in the ocean." She shrugged. "You aren't obligated to share anything with me. In fact—" she paused.

"What?"

She reluctantly admitted what she'd been thinking. "Given my connection to the man who had you tortured, perhaps we ought to go our separate ways."

Alec plodded through the sand after Lillian, pondering her suggestion. He didn't like it. Granted, she had a good point about keeping his distance from any connection to David Bardici, including his niece. But much as he knew, in his head, that her idea made sense, in his heart, he felt it was an awful plan.

If they split up, that would leave her alone and vulnerable. It would leave him alone. Worse than that, it would leave him without her. And he didn't want to be without her.

Night fell as they continued on their way, and Alec wrestled with the implications of his response to their situation. He had a duty to get back to Lydia, but he didn't know what he would find when he arrived there. Perhaps he ought to keep his distance until he knew more about what he was walking into.

"Perhaps," he suggested after walking in silence for over an hour, "you and I should stick together, precisely *because* of your connection to the general."

Lily stumbled, and he offered her the canteen. She looked beat.

"What do you mean?" Her hands shook as she held it to her lips.

"I don't know what's going on in Lydia. I don't know what your uncle is up to. Perhaps the quickest way to find out is through him."

Swallowing a sip, Lily handed back the canteen and looked thoughtful. Then her face brightened. "I could spy on him for you."

He couldn't help but grin at her change of demeanor, but at the same time, he cautioned her.

"Your uncle pulled a gun on you last night. I wouldn't want you to endanger yourself."

"I could be careful." She reached toward him as though to grab his arm as she had so many times during the last twenty-four hours, but then she looked self-conscious and shoved her hands into her pockets. "I could make him think I've had a change of heart. If he thought I was on his side, if he thought he could use me to get to you, perhaps, just maybe, I could convince him to reveal his plans to me."

Alec appreciated her willingness to help, but one thing bothered him. "Why would you do that for me?"

She looked confused. "I thought you said we were in this together?"

"But David Bardici is your uncle. I'm nothing to you. Why side with me instead of him?"

"You're the rightful prince. Your family was unjustly attacked by *my uncle*—the same man who put a gun to my throat."

"Do you think he had any intention of pulling the trigger?"

The shadows that flitted across her face looked all the more haunted in the moonlight. "Was the safety on or off?"

Alec didn't have to think. He recalled that detail with clarity. Though he'd replayed the scene in his mind a hundred times, wishing he'd simply ripped the gun from the general's hands, it would have been too risky under the circumstances. Lily could have been shot too easily, and he wasn't about to take chances on her life. Instead, he'd been forced to submit to the general's demands. "Off."

"So, he could have shot me. He could have stumbled when the boat rocked, or he could have twitched a little too much and I'd be dead?"

Unable to say the words out loud, Alec simply nodded.

"Then how can you ask why I'm siding with you over him?" she shouted into the empty night. "You pulled me out of the ocean when my leg was caught by the rope. You swung me around the precipice and didn't let me drop. You're sharing your water with me, even though keeping it to yourself would mean getting to civilization without dying of dehydration first."

She took a step closer and looked up into his face. "I owe you, Alec. I owe you for my life. More than that, my uncle threatened me, he tortured you. He deserves to pay. Are we in this together?"

Alec had to grin at Lillian's angry pledge of loyalty to him. "There's no one else I'd rather have on my side." He thought the words sounded corny when he spoke them, but as he hurried to keep up with Lily's determined march across the desert, he realized he meant them.

The cool of the desert night was a small comfort

as their trek grew longer, stretching on for endless miles, and the canteen he wore across his torso grew lighter as they emptied it. Soon they would be out of water. There was no sign of shelter ahead to keep the glaring sun off them during the heat of the day. A soldier couldn't make it more than a day in the desert without water. Lillian, in her exhausted condition, unaccustomed as she was to desert heat, wouldn't make it a fraction that long.

Alec swallowed back a sense of guilt. He hadn't led Lily into the desert to die. They'd had no choice—not unless they wanted to be captured by her uncle again.

The knot of guilt tightened in his chest. If they hadn't fled from David Bardici, Lillian would have a better chance of surviving. Would her uncle have tortured her? He couldn't know for sure, but their trek through the desert had to be torture enough for her.

The fine grains of sand shifted under his every step, fluctuating like his thoughts. Was it wise for them to head into the desert, not knowing when they might find water again? Or should he, for Lillian's sake, let them be captured again? At least then she'd probably get food and water.

But then, he didn't have the right to barter with his own life. He had a duty to the Lydian crown, and that duty hastened his every step. He couldn't let them be recaptured. He had to find his family.

Ridges of sand barred their path like small walls, each one an obstacle to be vaulted. Lillian had valiantly hurdled hundreds of them, but as the night wore on the formations grew more dramatic, the barriers higher. She wavered visibly as she faced a ridge of sand that came up past her knees.

Alec scooped her up in his arms, settling her back on her feet on the other side.

She made no sound but held on to him for just a second as she regained her balance. Her eyes met his, and she mouthed a thank-you before plodding on.

After a few more steps they met another ridge, and Alec lifted her over this one, as well.

Ridge after ridge, the sand, swept by endless desert winds, rippled ever higher, almost as though the desert resented their progress, as though the sand itself was trying to bar their way, and prevent them from going any farther. Alec knew enough of the North African sky to keep them headed southeast, as the stars waltzed a slow dance through the heavens in a timeless pattern that had guided many a desert caravan over the ages.

When they reached a ridge as high as Lily's waist, Alec did his best to swing his leg over, to step gracefully in spite of his exhaustion, but he underestimated the sand barrier, or overestimated his strength. Somehow, he caught his hip on the ridge and they tumbled down the soft side to the valley below.

He lay as he had landed, the sand prickling the scars on the left side of his face, the fine grains spilling into his nostrils, his ears, his eyes. It already filled his boots and every inch of his clothing, covering him, claiming him, threatening to bury him alive.

Lily crawled over and wiped his right cheek clear of sand. "Maybe we should just rest here for now." Her words slurred with exhaustion.

Alec closed his eyes, his body relaxing into the sand, the breeze pattering fine grains against them. If they stayed put, they'd be buried soon enough. "If your uncle sends men to check the wadi again, if any of our footprints weren't filled in with sand, and they realize we're headed south…" He paused to moisten his mouth, the words sticking in the dry heat. "They could come after us by helicopter, or on camels or horseback. It wouldn't take long for them to catch up to us. We'll be easy enough to spot in the open desert."

"Then we should get going," Lily said, but didn't move.

"If they catch up to us, they'll have water. He's your uncle. You'll be safe."

Her mouth hung open just a moment before she closed it against the blowing sand. "What about you? He'll torture you again."

"Will he? I might be able to escape. If I die out here, I won't be any help to my family."

"You're not going to die."

"Maybe we should go back toward the wadi. At least there we had water."

"No. We wouldn't make it anyway." She swallowed. "Not before the sun rises."

"What are we headed toward?"

"The blowing sand I saw."

"Was it a mirage?"

She lay silent in the sand for several long moments, until Alec began to fear she'd passed out from dehydration.

But then the stubborn woman spoke. "I'd rather die chasing a dream than giving up. The Rising Sun Horse Race runs somewhere ahead of us. As long as our trail leads toward it, I have hope. If we turn around—" her voice stilled, and it took her several moments to muster up the strength to finish her thought "—my uncle wins."

Alec understood. Pride and affection rose inside him, that Lillian would fight so valiantly, that she'd struggle on against all odds. He pushed himself to his knees, then to standing. When she clambered up next to him he held out his hand to help her up, and met her eyes.

"You'd make a good soldier." It was the highest compliment he could give her.

Her smile was weary, and he felt a tug of affection as she met his eyes. "Which way?"

"We can follow this valley a little longer. Maybe we'll find a lower ridge up ahead."

They made their way zigzagging along, down valleys, across ridges and down valleys again. Lillian increasingly leaned on him, and he was glad for it. Together they emptied the last few swallows of water from the canteen.

The ridges grew higher, until he couldn't see over them at all. Too soon the eastern sky grew sickly green, an ill portent of the desert's inevitable heat. He carried Lily up the next wall of sand, scooting down the other side and hauling them both to their feet.

Her head rested against his shirt, her weakening fingers clasping the thin fabric, a symbol of her tenuous hold on receding hope. He'd long ago accepted that they might not make it through the desert, but somewhere along the line, he'd tacitly vowed to keep trying for Lillian's sake. But before moving on, he let her hold on to him, let his arms wrap around her shoulders in something like an embrace.

As they'd trudged through the desert, his memory had returned in layers, peeling back like the ever-growing ridges they climbed. Holding her now, he picked through those memories for any inkling that there might have been another woman in his past, any other girl he'd held on to, not wanting to let her go.

There was no one. It came as bittersweet relief; sweet because he wanted Lily to be the only one, sorrowful because he didn't know how much longer they had together. Had the endless sands already buried his future, and hers?

She shifted against him, and he looked down to find her blinking up at him. "We should keep moving."

He brushed granules of sand from her cheek, tempted for a moment to kiss her. If they never made it out of the desert, he'd want to have kissed her before the end.

But they weren't beaten yet, and they had to keep moving. Bardici's men could come upon them at any time.

"This way."

They stumbled down the valley, their footprints dragging in a trail of exhaustion. If Bardici's men followed their footprints into the desert, their tiresome steps would read more clearly than a street sign, telling them they were losing strength. He and Lillian would be weak when the men caught up to them, the fight gone from their eyes, drained by the journey.

Lillian stumbled over nothing.

Alec reached for her, tried to grab her shoulder before she fell, but in his exhaustion, he moved too slowly. She caught herself on her knees, and he hauled her back up.

"Come on. Let's go over the ridge."

"It's too high," she protested.

He panted. The rising sun was warm, and the ridge was high—higher than any they'd yet encountered. "Over the ridge, there might be some shade. We can rest there out of the sun."

She nodded slowly, the motion more waver than assent. "When we get to the top, let's take a look around. Maybe we'll be able to see…" Her words faded.

He nodded, understanding. Maybe they could see…something other than sand, if there was anything other than sand anywhere to be seen.

The side of the ridge proved to be steep, and the shifting sand gave way with their every step, burying their feet as they went, weighing them down, until their hands flattened the wind-chiseled tip and they pulled themselves to standing.

Alec shaded his eyes as he peered across the glaring white.

Lily tugged on his arm. "There." She pointed farther east.

Sand billowed high into the air. Something was there—a herd of wild jackals, maybe, or a convoy of Bardici's men, but certainly *something*. They wouldn't know what it was until they made it over a few more ridges.

An eager grin cracked Lily's dried lips. "Let's go."

Even if he'd had the strength to caution her about running into whatever was ahead without scoping it out first, Alec wasn't about to dampen her hope. Hope was all the fuel they had left, and the billowing sand was still some distance away.

He took her hand and they charged forward.

Three mountainous ridges later, they pulled themselves up over a rocky lip and looked eastward toward the dusty cloud that continued to move beyond them. Between the cloud and their promontory, green branches waved skyward above a round pool, an oasis hidden between the ridges of sand.

"Praise God," Lily whispered.

"Yes," Alec agreed, though his eyes weren't on the water, but the caravans that camped there. The pond itself was a good sized one, more than thirty meters across, with date palms rimming the sides. Three distinct groups of men encamped at various points on its perimeter, all of them wearing traditional desert robes. The smallest group of Bedouins had only three men and two camels between them. Alec could see no weapons on them.

Another, larger group had close to a dozen camels stacked high with supplies. They appeared to have recently arrived, and were settling in against the heat of the day, the dark shadows of automatic rifles strapped across their backs. For protection? Or something less innocent?

The cluster that caught his attention was made up of at least four men with many more horses and camels. Their tents appeared to have weathered several nights at the oasis encampment, with the largest tent erected like a pavilion, its sides open to the desert air, its shadows full of objects Alec couldn't identify at such a distance.

Who were these nomads resting by the waterside? Were they friend or foe?

As he struggled to swallow, his mouth too dry and his tongue too swollen to permit anything more than breathing, Alec realized it didn't matter who the robe-cloaked men beyond them were. He and Lillian were simply too dehydrated to do anything but head for the water.

Whatever they encountered at the oasis, he'd have to quench his thirst before he could even defend them.

EIGHT

Lily wanted to hold Alec's hand for the sense of security it would give her, but the move would have been impractical, skidding as they were down the shifting sand, needing every limb at their disposal just to keep from going heels over head down the steep side of the dune. Besides, as she'd reminded herself throughout the night whenever she'd felt inclined to reach for him, he was royalty. There was probably a rule against touching him.

As they made their way gracelessly toward the oasis, the men camped there watched them curiously. No doubt they made quite a sight in their impractical clothes, without weapons or supplies.

A stretch of open water beckoned to them, far from the nearest group of men and their pavilion. Lily stumbled toward the water and fell facedown at its bank, plunging her whole head into the pond and letting the liquid splash into her mouth.

The water was cool and slightly sweet, apparently fed by an underground spring, and filtered by rocks and sand as it made its way to the surface. She swallowed greedily until the need for air forced her to lift her head. One gulping breath later, she plunged her head in again.

A hand touched her shoulder, and she looked up to see water glistening from the stubble on Alec's chin. "Don't drink too fast, or you'll make yourself sick. Let's get into the shade."

They shuffled toward the nearest palm trees, which brought them closer to the men near the pavilion, but thankfully, farther away from the gun-toting group across the way. Alec propped his back against a date-palm trunk.

Lily looked to do the same, but there wasn't a good spot near him, except for the other trunk that grew alongside his. She'd be rubbing shoulders with him if she rested there. Was she allowed to rub shoulders with the prince?

"What?" Alec squinted up at her. "Have a seat." He patted the ground beside him.

Self-consciously, Lillian eased her aching body toward the ground, leaning back and closing her eyes for a moment, letting the water revive her before attacking the task of removing her shoes and socks. With her feet finally freed, she padded barefoot the last few shaded feet to the water, rolled her khakis up past her ankles, and stepped in, dipping water by handfuls to drink.

She could feel the eyes of the Bedouin men on her, but she was far too thirsty to care what they were thinking. Were any of them working for her uncle? If so, they weren't making their move yet. Alec stepped into the water beside her, and she relaxed at his protective presence. They were grossly outnumbered and outgunned, but the prince of Lydia had proven himself to be a match for any foe. She pitied anyone who would be rash enough to assault him.

After drinking her fill again, she walked back to the palm trees and settled into her spot, closing her eyes only after Alec joined her.

How long she rested, only half-asleep, but blissfully motionless, she couldn't guess. In fact, she'd nearly nodded off in earnest when her subconscious was pricked with the realization that they weren't alone.

Lily opened her eyes to see a large black gun dangling from a man's hand in front of her.

He spoke. Lily couldn't make out anything of what he said—it certainly wasn't in English. But Alec responded with like-sounding words, and the man gestured with his gun toward the pavilion.

It didn't seem to be a threatening gesture. The Bedouin rubbed his thumb against his fingers. Money?

Alec nodded and stood, pointed to Lily, said something more to the man.

The stranger nodded agreeably, waving with the gun in a welcoming manner, though Lillian wasn't at all used to being welcomed by a waving gun. When Alec extended a hand toward her, she let him pull her up, and they walked barefoot along the shaded ground toward the tent pavilion.

She smiled at what she saw inside. Besides traditional date cakes and pistachios, there were bottled sodas, packaged snacks, folded clothing, blankets, canteens, binoculars and pocket knives. "It's a store?" she whispered to Alec.

The Bedouin stepped back, watching them from the doorway but otherwise letting them browse freely.

"He's a vendor, catering to the riders and spectators of the Rising Sun Horse Race," Alec explained. "The course passes by here. The clouds you saw to the east are riders trying to cover as much distance as possible before the heat of the day makes travel impossible. That small band of men on the far side of the oasis are relatives of one of the racers, stopping here while they watch his progress."

"And the larger band, the men with guns?"

Alec shrugged. "A caravan of nomads, just stopping to rest, I hope."

"Why so many weapons?"

"The desert is a dangerous place."

"They look like dangerous men." Even as she

spoke the words, Lily reminded herself that Alec was an equally dangerous man, guns or no guns. He picked up a few candy bars and a large bottle of fruity soda, its label unfamiliar to her, though the promise of sugary refreshment was familiar enough.

Hunger clawed at her stomach, but Lily was reluctant to reach for the tempting snacks. She didn't have any money. In fact, she was deep in debt after her parents had surprised her with the news that they weren't paying for her veterinary schooling after all. Alec had already carried her over dozens of dunes—she owed him a debt of gratitude already. She hated to depend on his charity, especially when she had no way of paying him back, even if they made it out of the desert.

Alec leaned over her shoulder. "Can't make up your mind?"

She sighed as she turned to face him. "I have no money."

He scowled. "We're in this together. I've got it covered."

"No." She shook her head, resenting the words and the bitter truth that forced her to speak them. "I have *no* money—none anywhere. Even if I get back to the U.S., I don't have anything but debt. I have no way of paying you back."

Alec's scowl morphed from offended to confused. "Your parents' yacht—"

"Is the last thing they own that they haven't sold." She finished his sentence. "They've sold all their properties, they stopped paying my school bills, even though they told me before I started school that they'd cover all the expenses." Lily bit her lip. This wasn't the time or the place to spill her troubles, but she felt her resentment rising up inside her. She'd have taken a job, maybe even interrupted her studies had she known... But she hadn't known.

Alec must have sensed her feelings. "Pick out something to eat. Then we're going to sit down and you're going to tell me about it."

"You don't need to trouble yourself with my problems."

"Who says they're *your* problems?" Alec's voice dropped to a whisper, and he bent his head close so they couldn't be overheard. "Your father is David Bardici's brother. What are your folks doing with the money they've made from the sales?"

"I don't know. It's disappeared."

"The general doesn't make enough to fund a war. He's getting support from somewhere." Alec's jaw clenched. "Your problems are my problems. They're all of Lydia's problems. I need to know everything, because right now, I know nothing."

His words cut through her hunger-dulled consciousness. Had her parents funded the attack on Alec's family? The thought was enough to wipe out her appetite, but Lily obediently reached for a candy bar. They had a long way to go, and she'd need her strength if she was going to tell Alec anything. She dreaded sharing anything about the past she'd tried so hard to forget.

Alec pulled a few bills from the money clip without removing the cash from his pocket. It wouldn't do to let anyone see how much money he was carrying. As a soldier, he'd been warned about desert bandits. Without the protection of a gun and armed comrades, he and Lily were particularly vulnerable.

The man who'd first approached them counted out change, while another sat in the shade with a crank-style radio near his ear, the broadcast in Arabic. Alec was only marginally fluent in the written language, but he could speak Arabic fluently, and knew more than enough to clearly understand the news report that crackled over the airwaves. They were talking about the situation in Lydia.

The Bedouin handed him change, Alec nodded his thanks, and then stepped closer to the radio to hear.

The news report told the story of what had happened two days before in Sardis. The royal motorcade had been ambushed. The members of the royal family were unaccounted for, but in the latest twist in the story, Princess Isabelle was meeting with Parliament.

Alec wanted to give a loud whoop for joy at the news that his sister was alive and apparently well enough to meet with Parliament, but he didn't want to show his reaction. There was no telling who the men were whose camps encircled the oasis or where their allegiances lay. He couldn't risk showing any emotion in front of them.

As the broadcast moved on to the next story, Alec thanked the merchant again and headed back to the shade of the date palms with Lily at his side. Before they settled down, she asked him, "What did you hear on the radio that made you so happy?"

Immediately alarmed that he may have given away more than he'd intended, he asked, "How did you know the news on the radio made me happy?"

"Your eyes lit up. You got a spring in your step."

Alec hoped the merchants would attribute his response to his happiness about their purchases, and not any personal stake in the Lydian government. There was nothing he could do to go back in time and erase his reaction. But he was eager to share the report with Lily.

"The radio broadcast was an update on the situation in Lydia. My sister Isabelle is meeting with Parliament."

"That means she must have escaped the attack. Oh, thank God. Did they mention the rest of your family?"

"Only that they were unaccounted for."

"That has to be good news, right?"

"I hope so." He unwrapped a candy bar, then paused, overwhelmed by gratitude. Less than half an hour before, he'd thought they were doomed to die in the desert and had every reason to believe his entire family had been killed, as well.

Lily must have felt the same impulse he did. "We should give thanks."

He agreed and reached for her hand, though she seemed to hesitate before placing her small palm in his. Then he closed his eyes and thanked God, not just for providing them with food and water and shade, but also for watching over his sister. He asked God to keep the rest of his family safe, but when he thanked God for sending Lily to help him, he felt her pull back. After a quick "amen," he popped his eyes open and caught her guilty expression.

"What?" He tore into his candy bar, and popped the top on the soda.

"Don't thank God for bringing me into your life. My family has got to be your worst nightmare." She looked down at the candy bar in her hands, which she hadn't bothered to unwrap.

"Eat it before it melts."

But Lily looked sick to her stomach. "I couldn't

imagine what my dad was doing with all his money, but your theory makes perfect sense. Why didn't I figure it out sooner? Why didn't I pay more attention when my dad and Uncle David talked about Lydian politics?"

"I doubt they would have been careless enough to discuss the attack on the motorcade around you." He reached over and opened her candy bar for her. "Besides, from what I understand, your father didn't realize the attack would take place when it did. He'd been told to leave town before the state dinner. If he would have realized the danger of letting you watch the motorcade pass by, he would have set sail sooner."

As he spoke, Alec glanced across the oasis at the other camps. The men with the guns were sitting up straighter. Alec kept his head down, but watched them out of the corner of his eye. They had a radio. Most likely they'd heard the same broadcast, and had seen the spring in his step when his sister was mentioned. Did they know David Bardici? Had Lily's uncle—clearly a powerful man in the region—already put out word for folks to be looking for them? Was there even now a bounty on their heads?

One of the men pulled out a cell phone, but he didn't put it to his ear. Instead, he held it up facing them, before a satisfied look crossed his face and he retreated into one of their tents.

Glancing back at Lily, Alec saw her resolutely chewing a bite of candy bar, though she looked as though she might have been crying, had she not been too dehydrated to shed tears.

"Eat quickly," he warned her. "As soon as you finish, we're going to pick out horses from the merchants."

"Horses?"

"The Bedouin told me his horses are for sale." Alec quickly calculated how long they might have before Bardici's men reached them, assuming the man in the tent texted a picture of them from his phone. He'd noticed a cell-phone tower extending above the walls of Bardici's fortress, no doubt supplying coverage to the area.

If Bardici's men came by helicopter, they could arrive in a little over an hour. There was no time to waste. "We have to get out of here. One of those men just used his cell phone to take our picture. If he suspects who we are." Alec shook his head, already regretting that he hadn't been more cautious. "We don't have much time. Let's move."

Lily shoved the last bite of candy bar into her mouth and reached for her shoes. She hadn't been looking forward to explaining anything more to Alec about her family, but she'd have gladly traded that conversation for the journey ahead of them. Neither of them had yet had an opportunity to sleep.

"Where are we going to go?" she asked as she tied on her sneakers. "If we head back the way we came, they'll only find us sooner. In fact, no matter where we go, we'll be easy to find in the open desert."

"We'll follow the race course," Alec interjected. "If we're on horses, no one will suspect we're not one of the racers unless they get close enough to see our faces."

Her shoes on, Lily hurried toward where the horses grazed on the sparse grass near the oasis. As she'd feared when she'd first spotted them from a distance, most of the horses looked exhausted. "Were these animals traded in by the racers?"

Alec had apparently already discussed the horses with the merchant. "The race only follows the riders. They're allowed to switch animals over the course of the race. These traders have made a bundle, and picked up some nice stock in the process."

While Lily agreed that the horses appeared to be well-bred, most of them with significantly more Arabian blood in their veins than the "Arabian" horses she'd encountered in America, they had obviously been ridden hard in the last few days, and hadn't been at the oasis nearly long enough to recover from the ordeal. They looked beat.

"I'll look for some decent animals," she told Alec. "You sort out what we can afford to buy."

"I'll pick up the supplies we'll need, too."

Lily nodded, but her attention was already on the horses, most of which were too tired to even look up as she approached. Not a good sign. They wouldn't make it much farther in this heat—and she was quite certain Alec wasn't about to let them rest for the remainder of the midday sun. If they were going to stay ahead of her uncle's men, they'd have to strike out at the least opportune time.

By the time Alec and the Bedouin joined her, she'd picked out her most likely candidates. "This fellow looks like he can hold you." She stroked the neck of a massive red roan gelding who appeared, from his coloring and awesome size, to have Belgian draft horse blood somewhere not too far back in his ancestry. "He doesn't appear to be as tired as the rest, either."

Alec and the merchant exchanged words, and the prince smiled his approval. "You have a good eye. This horse was never in the race. He's bred to carry heavy loads, not for speed. An excellent choice." Alec patted the animal on the neck.

The merchant tried to recommend a couple of other animals, but Lily led them to the one she'd selected for herself, a dappled gray filly whose high-arched tail and mane were as white as the desert sand. The animal raised her delicate head as they approached, and snorted at them, as though warning them away.

"She's pure Arabian," Lily marveled, extending her hand toward the spirited animal.

Immediately the merchant began talking to Alec, and though Lily didn't understand a word of Arabic, she wasn't surprised when Alec informed her of what the man had said.

"She's still wild, Lily. They can't even get a saddle on her. She's only ever been halterbroke."

"I'll ride bareback."

"You can't."

She looked up at him and grinned. "I've been doing it since I was twelve, when I begged my father to give me a horse allowance. He was stingy even then, so in order to afford more than one, I bought yearlings and broke them myself. If I couldn't get a saddle on them, I rode bareback until they adjusted to having me around." The memories welled up as she spoke, and she caught herself before she said too much.

"An unbroken horse is a liability," Alec argued, "one we can't afford right now."

"None of the rest of these animals have the strength to make a hard ride after what they've already been through. I know she's got spirit. That spirit might be our strongest asset when it comes to getting out of this desert." She saw his resolve weakening, and she grinned up at him. "Besides, riding bareback will save us the cost of another saddle."

Alec shook his head. "We don't have time to argue about this."

"Perfect. Can we afford two horses, along with everything else?" She gestured to the pile of supplies Alec had accumulated, including several canteens of water.

"It will drain all our funds. We'll be down to enough money for a few meals, maybe hotel rooms if we ever reach a town, but we won't be able to afford plane tickets."

"We don't have passports anyway."

Alec let out a resigned sigh. "Try to get on her first. If she throws you, you'll have to pick another animal."

"Thank you." Lily felt so delighted, she nearly hugged him, but caught herself just as she threw her arms up. Alec met her eyes, and for an instant she suspected he knew what she'd been about to do. Rather than think about her increasingly complicated feelings for the man, she untied the rope that bound the filly to a date palm, and led her to an open stretch of sand.

One of the Bedouins, his face alight with the prospect of seeing her attempt to mount the horse, trotted out with a mounting block and set it on a level spot. He nodded to her with sporting challenge dancing in his eyes.

She led the prancing horse to the spot, and ran a hand down her neck, murmuring her plans in a soothing monologue. "We're going to show these men what we can do, girl. We're going to get out of here and run free. Are you ready to run?" Nervous energy rippled under her palm. "Yes, you're ready to run."

Lily got up on the block and leaned her upper body across the filly's back. The animal pranced backward, and Lily stumbled off the block, knocking it sideways. She set it upright and met Alec's eyes.

"We don't have time to mess around," he warned her, his expression more concerned than impatient.

She couldn't help grinning at him, the thrill of working the fantastic filly overpowering any chagrin she might have felt. "Have you got your horse saddled? When we take off, you might have to hurry to keep up."

Alec took the warning seriously, and while Lily leaned on the filly again, letting the animal grow accustomed to her presence and some of her weight, Alec paid for their purchases and prepped the Belgian for the ride. Then she offered to put some of their food and water supplies on her horse.

"You don't even have a saddle," Alec reminded her. "Let's see if she'll even carry you."

"Mount up," Lily suggested as Alec secured the last of their supplies to his horse.

He raised an eyebrow at her.

"Get ready to go. When I go, there won't be

any waiting. In fact, you might want to get a head start." Lily could feel the nervous energy of the Arabian filly. The animal sensed that something was about to happen, and Lily knew enough to guess how the horse would react once she jumped on her back. She'd have her hands full just holding on, and hopefully keeping her pointed in the right direction, though the oasis valley was rimmed on both sides by steep sand dunes, so other than going backward, there was little chance her horse would try to run in any direction other than the one she wanted her to go.

Alec grinned. "I'd hate to miss the show."

Lily gauged the filly's readiness with her hand on the horse's neck. The animal's pulse was leveling off slightly. She wasn't quite so nervous. Now was her shot. "Don't blink," she told Alec, before swinging a leg over the filly's back.

The animal reared before she got her leg all the way over, but Lily held tight to the rope halter and put her weight on the filly's neck. "You didn't mean that," she whispered toward the horse's ear.

As if to prove she had, the Arabian took off down the valley, her speed from the start something to be reckoned with. If Alec was behind her, he'd have his hands full just keeping her within sight.

The filly tore up the ground as she pounded in a dappled streak down the desert, the soft sand flying behind her. Tears streaked from Lily's eyes as the wind tore into her face. She stayed tight to the filly's neck, high on her shoulders, gripping the galloping steed with her knees and swallowing back the whoop of exhilaration that rose within her.

She hadn't been on a horse in months—hadn't thought she'd ever want to ride a horse again after watching her father's herd die, but the fantastic animal beneath her changed her mind. They sped through the desert until Lily thought the filly would have to slow down or collapse from the effort.

Not that she was about to complain about the speed. She knew the threat of her uncle's approach was sincere. There was no other reason for the bandits to take their picture. She and Alec had no choice but to stay well ahead of her uncle's men.

Gradually, the sprinting horse eased her speed to a natural gallop, and Lily settled back, relaxing the tight knot in her shoulders, and turning her head to see how far Alec had fallen behind. She peered down the endless expanse of white sand, which seemed to stretch out behind her forever.

Alec was nowhere to be seen.

NINE

As Alec watched Lily's slender figure clinging to the half-wild horse as it tore off from the oasis encampment, he couldn't help but be impressed by Lillian's skill and courage. Besides that, the fine animal and rider were a picture of beauty as they sped through the barren desert.

Realizing he'd have to hurry just to keep up, Alec hauled himself onto his patiently waiting draft horse, giving the animal a gentle prod with his heels to get him started. The horse clearly understood. Perhaps inspired by Lillian's amazing show of speed, he accelerated to a canter as they made their way around the curving ridge of sand. Far ahead he could see Lillian's figure clinging like a burr to the streak of silver lightning she rode.

With his attention focused on Lillian's horsemanship, Alec didn't notice the stealthily approaching Bedouins until two of them, in a coordinated attack, pulled up even with him on either side, automatic rifles balanced across their horses' withers, muzzles pointed at him.

A glance behind revealed three more armed men on horseback, and the man who'd surreptitiously taken his picture riding close to his heels. Alec considered trying to sprint ahead, but any of the other horses could have likely outrun his, even if the draft horse hadn't been weighed down with supplies. And the guns pointed his way clearly meant business.

He slowed, and addressed the men in Arabic. "Can I help you?"

"You're coming with us."

Alec reined in his horse almost to a stop. "Surely we can discuss this." As he prepared to dismount, he made careful note of each man's position. Granted, he was outnumbered and outgunned, but Lillian was alone in the desert without water, on a horse she couldn't really control. He didn't have time to be captured and escape. The men would have to be dispensed with quickly.

But he also wanted to know how much they knew. "Do you men know who I am?"

"You're my next paycheck." The Bedouin who'd taken his picture held up the generous-size screen in his hand, revealing a picture of Alec preinjury, with a caption promising a reward for his capture, the bounty equal to nearly twenty-thousand American dollars—more than the average North African made in a year. The leering man leaned toward him.

Lily felt a rising sense of panic as she strained to see behind her. The Arabian horse had slowed her pace somewhat, but she was still at a full gallop, and focusing on anything was nearly impossible. There was no sign of the oasis in the distance, either. Apparently the valley of sand they were following had curved around enough that the spring and all its trees had bent completely out of sight.

Telling herself Alec was surely just around the bend and would reappear any moment, Lily kept the horse on her forward course. She had little say in the matter. Tugging on the halter only produced an impatient shake of the animal's head, whipping the white mane back into her eyes. *Eventually* the filly had to tire. Didn't she?

Glancing back several more times without seeing anything but endless white sand, Lily began to wonder if she'd somehow gone off course after all. But wouldn't Alec simply follow her footprints and find her? Surely the gentle desert breeze didn't fill them in that quickly, did it?

Another terror seized her. What if Alec had been captured by her uncle? The men at the oasis had taken his picture, and presumably sent it to her uncle. The men might have been instructed to grab Alec. Was he even now being held by her uncle's armed men?

Lily pulled back on the halter, trying to stop the horse, or at least turn her around. "Whoa, girl. We need to stop. We have to go back." Tears filled her eyes. "*Please.* My friend is back there. We need to make sure he's okay."

Wrapping her arms around the horse's neck, Lily pulled back. The animal fought her, and her pace slowed, but only slightly.

Lily's thoughts raced. She could throw herself down from the horse—the soft sand would cushion her fall enough that she might escape injury—except that then she'd be alone in the desert, without a horse, with no water and no supplies, and the spirited animal had already sprinted for several miles. She might not make it back to the oasis until sundown. Her uncle could have taken Alec anywhere by then.

As she tried to think of what to do, a large shape appeared in the distance ahead of her. Unsure what to make of it at first, Lillian realized as they drew closer that is was a rock formation, jutting up from the desert like the ridges of the wadi, but alone in the sand, far from any other rock formations.

There didn't appear to be anything growing near

it, no spring to water any plants, but the looming shape offered shade, and the midafternoon sun beat down mercilessly.

"There, girl. There's shade up ahead. Let's rest there. It will be cooler there."

To her relief, the animal must have felt the same need for cool shade that she did, because she made her way toward the rock, slowing to a canter and then a walk, before coming to a complete stop in the shadow of the formation that stretched high above their heads.

Lily panted, patting the horse and wiping the sweat from her neck. "Good girl." She soothed the animal and tried to think of what her next move should be. Much as she wanted to get the horse pointed back in the direction they'd come, no amount of urging would nudge her from her spot in the shade.

Finally, Lily leaned forward and rested against the Arabian's high-arched neck. All she could think of was Alec, and how badly she wanted to know that he was okay. She turned her head to face the direction from which they'd come, and though she could see her horse's footprints stretching out into the distance, there was no sign of Alec anywhere.

"Oh, dear God," she prayed, biting back tears. "Please help Alec. Help him be okay." The words sounded familiar, and she recalled the last time she'd prayed such a prayer—for her father's horses. And they'd all ended up dead.

Painful as that experience had been, she realized Alec meant far more to her than the beloved animals. He was brave and strong and, though she knew he was a prince and far out of her league, she couldn't help the feelings she had for him.

Strong feelings. "Please, God," she whispered, pinching back her tears, wrapping her arms around the filly's neck, as much to keep her tired body from slipping off as for comfort, "please let me see Alec again. Keep him safe."

The horse beneath her nickered almost as though she understood, and Lily sighed, letting her tired body relax slightly. She hadn't slept since her brief nap the morning before, and between her dehydrated wanderings and the frantic sprint on horseback, sleep tugged at her from all directions.

"Please, God," she whispered again, not bothering to open her eyes, or even climb off the horse. After all, if she climbed off the horse, the animal might wander away and leave her. She couldn't risk that, even though there was nothing more she could do to force herself to stay awake. Exhaustion reached its determined hands toward her. She would have liked to fight it, to stay awake long enough to search for Alec, but the heat and the long ride had stolen the last of her strength.

* * *

Alec sized up the photograph quickly, and caught just enough of the terms beneath his picture to know the men were required to bring him in alive if they wanted to collect.

At least that was one thing in his favor.

"Are you sure you've got the right man?" Alec leaned forward as though to inspect the picture. At the last second he turned his horse sideways, blocking the three men behind from reaching him, and vaulted from the saddle, slamming his would-be kidnapper midchest with his boots. The man keeled backward from his horse while Alec grabbed the rifle from its withers, whipping the stock toward the mounted horseman on the other side, slamming him backward as the man scrambled to point his own gun at him. His horse reared up, throwing him.

Alec pointed the rifle at the remaining men, who gripped their guns and eyed him uneasily, as though unsure, after his show of power, whether the three of them ought to take him on.

The man who'd fallen first yelled at them from the ground, demanding in angry Arabic that they go after Alec.

The rider nearest him spurred his horse around, but before he got the animal facing him, Alec sent one shot into the man's saddle horn.

With a whinnying scream, his mount panicked,

throwing himself backward toward the other two horses, who bolted in the direction of the oasis, quickly followed by the frightened animal whose saddle horn he'd nicked.

Alec swung around to face the other two men. The second man had managed to get back on his horse again, and rode off after his fleeing comrades. The first of his attackers, the one with the tablet that held his picture, shuffled backward in the sand.

Alec grabbed him by the shoulders and hauled him to his feet. "Who's offering the bounty?" he asked in Arabic.

"Bardici." The man pointed to the north, as though indicating the direction toward the Bardici compound.

"What do you know about him?"

The man shook his head. "His money is good."

"What can you tell me about his compound? How many men does he have?"

"I don't know. Many men—armed, trained soldiers. Many armed guards."

"Have you been to his compound?"

"I've seen it. It's surrounded by high walls, on cliffs overlooking the sea."

Alec knew from experience that the Bedouin's description was correct. "How do they come and go? Are there any roads?"

"One road through to Benghazi. The men go back and forth. Also helicopters and boats."

"Is there a pier?"

The man nodded. "On the northeast side, almost a kilometer from the compound. It's the only spot away from the rocks."

"Good." Alec took the man's phone. It was an impressive newer model phone with a large screen, clearly quite expensive.

Grabbing the man's rifle and the handgun he carried in a holster at his hip, Alec shoved the Bedouin back in the direction of the oasis. "If Bardici finds out you let me get away, he will be angry. Don't wait for him to find you. Run."

The man fled on foot through the sand in the direction his comrades and horse had gone.

Alec turned to his own mount. He had no guarantees the men wouldn't report to Bardici, but he felt confident the man understood his threat, and anyway, he planned to be gone long before David Bardici or any of his men arrived.

Turning his horse in the direction Lillian had traveled, he nudged the beast back up to a canter and picked up the quickly filling tracks her sprinting horse had left behind. How far had Lily already traveled? Would his much-slower mount ever catch up to her?

His chest tightened at the thought of Lillian running into trouble without him. Not only did her uncle obviously have a long arm, but the desert held plenty of other threats, from poisonous snakes to raiding bandits. But most unmercifully of all the heat that beat down on the endless sand. And Alec knew Lily had no water.

The thought of her suffering spurred him forward, though exhaustion clawed relentlessly at his dry eyes. He'd promised Lily he would keep her safe, but more than that, his pounding heart threatened to burst at the thought of anything happening to her. He recalled the way she'd stubbornly insisted on moving forward, refusing to give up hope even when his hope had dimmed. He couldn't fail her.

Besides, he'd wanted for some time to kiss her, and told himself he would before the desert defeated them.

"Come on, boy." He prodded the horse onward, the thought of kissing Lillian spurring him forward even more than the threats that lay behind him.

The sun had rounded the dome of the sky and the shadows darkened every ripple of sand when Alec's bleary eyes caught sight of a shape in front of him. Through the haze of heat he made out a rock formation, with a horse and rider planted unmoving beneath.

Lillian.

He urged his horse to a gallop, his eyes never

once leaving her face. Was she okay? She wasn't moving. Had she passed out? Was the heat too much for her? With growing concern, he recalled from his training the grim prognosis for heatstroke. Without immediate medical treatment, even a seasoned soldier could die quickly after the onset of symptoms.

Alec surveyed the way Lillian slumped against her horse's neck. She didn't raise her eyes at his approach, or make the slightest move to indicate she was conscious, or even alive.

Slowing his horse as they approached, Alec slid from the saddle, still gripping the reins, and put a hand to Lillian's forehead. She didn't feel cool and clammy—which would have been an awful sign. She didn't feel frighteningly hot, but neither did she twitch at his touch.

Quickly looping his horse's reins through the Arabian's simple rope halter, he secured the animals together and wrapped his arms around Lillian's limp body, pulling her down from the horse.

She slumped against him, and her eyelids fluttered as her cheek rested against his chest.

He grabbed a bottle of soda from his saddlebag and tipped the strawberry-flavored liquid to her lips. It pooled in her mouth before she sputtered, then swallowed.

Her eyes opened.

"Another drink?" he offered.

She looked disoriented, but opened her mouth, and he raised the bottle to her lips. She took a few more sips, then shifted against him, putting some of her weight on her feet. "More?" She reached for the bottle.

He handed it to her, but warned, "Slowly."

While she quenched her thirst, he opened a canteen and downed several gulps. It had been a long day, and a long ride, but not even the taste of water was as much a relief to him as the sight of Lily leaning against him, sipping strawberry soda.

She looked up at him and let out a sigh, her strawberry-scented breath enticing him.

"Are you okay?" he asked.

"I think so. I was worried about you. What happened?"

"The men who took our picture followed me. Seems your uncle David has put a price on my head."

Concern filled her features and she opened her mouth as though to apologize again.

Alec leaned down and, before she could say anything, he kissed her.

The move must have caught her by surprise, because she froze a full second before kissing him back.

He wrapped his arms around her and pulled her closer. Her kisses were more refreshing than the water at the oasis after their long journey through the desert, and far more intoxicating. Relief at finding her unharmed combined with the attraction he'd been denying through the journey, made her irresistible.

Besides, she certainly seemed to be enjoying kissing him.

It wasn't until the horses snorted impatiently that Alec remembered they didn't have time for such indulgences. Bardici's men might find them at any time.

Reluctantly, he took a step back, leaving a final, light kiss on the tip of her nose as he pulled himself away. "We need…" He cleared his throat, trying to think, half tempted to take her in his arms again.

But Lillian seemed to grasp the situation, as well. "I'm sorry, I shouldn't…" She raised her fingers as though to erase the kiss, but then seemed to realize she couldn't, or didn't want to.

"Shouldn't?" he questioned. "I started it."

"But you're royalty."

"And?"

"I probably shouldn't even touch you, should I?"

The sincere trepidation on her face made him smile. "Is that why you've been pulling your hands back every time you start to reach for me?"

Her blush told him she'd hoped he hadn't noticed.

He wanted to kiss her again, but didn't think

he'd have the strength to pull himself away a second time. "You don't need to keep your distance." He still had her mostly in his arms, which only reinforced his point.

Still, she looked unconvinced. "But our families are enemies."

"That doesn't change how I feel about you." He watched as her eyes widened. "Does it influence your feelings toward me?"

"Only that I feel awful for what my uncle has done."

Glad that she hadn't denied her apparent affection for him, nonetheless, at the mention of the general, Alec was reminded of all that still lay ahead of them. "I need to sort out how your family is connected to the attack on my family. Night is falling. We can talk while we travel."

"Where are we going?"

"North."

"But…" Lillian took a half step back from him and looked around, as if verifying her bearings. "After we left my uncle's fortress, we traveled southwest, and now east again. If we go north we'll end up at his doorstep."

"Precisely."

"But—"

Alec pulled her close again, shushing her. "I spoke with one of the men who tried to capture me. There's a pier nearly a kilometer up the shoreline from your uncle's estate. I can't help but think that your parents will be sailing toward there. David probably gave them the location. If they've made decent time, they should arrive some time tomorrow."

"What are you suggesting?"

"I'm not sure, exactly, but I'd like to get back to Sardis, learn what's happening there, find my sister and maybe the rest of my family."

"How does heading to my uncle's compound accomplish that?"

"Your parents have a boat. We've already determined we're not going to get through any airports or across any borders without money or passports." He grinned at her. "How good are you at sailing?"

"I can sail my parents' yacht all by myself, if that's what you're asking, but Alec—"

He silenced her protests with a kiss, then pulled back just far enough to meet her eyes. "Do you trust me?"

A smile spread across her lips. "More than anyone."

He couldn't help grinning back as an odd, giddy sensation rippled through him. No one had ever made him feel like this before. Was this what it felt like to be in love? Now he understood why entire nations had fallen over the love of a woman. It was a powerful force, and made him feel as though he could cross the desert and back again just to be with Lillian.

He planted another kiss on her lips—this time, a kiss of promise. "It will all be all right. We need to get going."

Lillian helped water the horses and shared a quick snack with Alec before they got on their way. Though she knew her body ought to be begging to rest, she felt almost as though she was dancing on air, and kept stealing glances at Alec as he worked, trading goofy grins with him every time she caught him looking her way.

Granted, he was a prince far outside of her league, and apparently the members of her extended family were out to overthrow his family and maybe kill them, but that didn't change the way she felt about him. And if his kisses were any indication, he felt the same way. If she'd had wings, she could have flown them back to Sardis.

Instead, as the sun dipped below the horizon and they pointed their horses north, Lillian worked up the courage to tell Alec everything she knew about her family history, including the painful details of her immediate past. She began with the Bardicis' link to Lydia.

"My uncle David and my father were both born in Lydia, though they also had joint American citizenship, since both their parents were American.

The way I understand it, my grandfather Bardici was an American businessman. My grandmother was the one with ties to Lydia. She's the reason they moved to Lydia before their sons were born."

"What was her name?"

"Helen. Before she married my grandfather, her last name was Valli, but I believe that was her first husband's last name. Her maiden name was…" Lily watched the endless sand ripple under the moonlight as she tried to recall. "That's strange."

"What is?"

"I think her maiden name was *Lydia*. But that doesn't make any sense, does it?" Even as she questioned her memory, Lillian couldn't help thinking of the name badge Alec had worn above his medals on his soldier's uniform the day she'd rescued him from the ambush.

"There are people in Lydia who have the last name Lydia."

"Are there?"

"Yes," Alec assured her. "All those who belong to the Royal House of Lydia use *Lydia* as their surname. If your grandmother's last name was Lydia, she must have been a member of the royal family."

TEN

"That can't be right." Lillian was grateful the horse she rode kept moving forward at a steady clip. If it had been up to her to keep herself moving, she'd have certainly stumbled. "How could my grandmother possibly be part of the royal family?" But even as she asked the question, she recalled snippets of conversations she'd overheard years before. Maybe it wasn't so impossible.

"My father Philip was an only child," Alec explained. "His father, who was also king before him, was the oldest of three. His two younger sisters married foreigners, but neither of them went to America, and neither of them were named Helen. We get Christmas cards from them every year."

"My grandmother passed away eight years ago."

"Then she can't be the same person as either of my great aunts." Alec looked thoughtful. "You say your grandmother Helen also had American citizenship? Where was she born?"

"In America, I believe. Her mother was from Greece and her father from Lydia."

"What was her father's name?"

Lillian tried to recall. "It was something foreign, almost British-sounding."

"Basil?" Alec pulled his horse up short.

"Yes." Lillian halted her mount as well as Alec slid from his saddle and knelt over an open stretch of sand that glimmered white in the moonlight.

"My great-grandfather's name was Alexander." Alec used the tip of his finger to draw a large *A* in the sand. "I'm named after him, so I studied quite a bit of his life story. He had an older half brother named Basil." Alec sketched a *B* in the sand near the *A* he'd drawn.

Lillian felt her heart beating hard. If Alexander's great-grandfather wasn't the oldest, then why did his family inherit the throne?

Alec continued. "Basil's mother died when he was born. His father remarried some years later, but Basil never liked his stepmother and didn't get along well with the family. His grandfather was king then—he lived to a ripe old age—and his father was only a prince. Perhaps Basil never thought the throne would pass to him, or perhaps he didn't care, but he abdicated and ran off to America to marry a Greek actress. He died a few years later. It seems to me that he had a daughter before he died, though."

As he explained his family history, Alec drew a line from Basil and put an *H* below it. "If Basil's daughter is your grandmother, Helen, that would explain why she had the last name *Lydia*—because she was a descendent of the royal house of Lydia."

Lillian bent next to the rough family tree Alec had etched in the sand. Under her grandmother's *H* she placed a *D* and *M.* "David and Michael—my uncle and father."

"Do you have any cousins?"

"Uncle David has never married. I'm an only child." She drew a line from the *M* and wrote an *L* to signify herself. Then she looked at the large empty patch under the letter *A.* "Where do you come in?"

"King Alexander was my great-grandfather. He came to the throne during World War One, and reigned for over sixty years. My grandfather was crowned in 1978 and reigned until he and his wife were killed in a helicopter crash eight years ago. That's when my father ascended to the throne." Alec drew four lines below his father's name, marking them with a *T, A, I,* and another *A.*

"Thaddeus, Alexander, Isabelle, Anastasia." He named them off as he drew them in.

Lily had to take a step back to take in the whole scope of the family tree. It looked like a complicated mess to her, each line of succession a tiny dividing wall of hostility between Alec's family and hers. "Basil and Alexander." She named the half brothers. "But it was so long ago. You wouldn't think anyone would care anymore."

"There's a throne at stake. Perhaps your uncle and father feel that's still worth caring about."

"We should keep moving," she told him, hoping he'd help boost her onto the back of her horse so they could leave the family tree far behind them.

Instead, Alec stepped close.

"What is it, Lillian?" He traced her cheekbone with his finger, and tipped her chin up gently until she looked in his eyes. "Something about this family tree bothers you."

"Doesn't it bother you? My great-grandfather walked away from the throne, and now my father and uncle seem intent on getting it back." She looked at the letters in the sand while her eyes filled with tears, bits and pieces of things her father and uncle had said the week before now coming back to her with decoded meaning. She wished she could deny the truth of it, to erase it as easily as a swipe of her foot would erase the initials etched in the sand, but ultimately she knew truth was truth, regardless of her feelings about it. "It all makes sense now, doesn't it? That's why they attacked your family. That's why—" She gasped as the pieces fell into place.

"What?"

"Your grandfather and grandmother died in a helicopter accident. What caused it?"

"Mechanical malfunction." His jaw tightened. "You don't think it was an accident?"

Lillian looked up at the stars blinking brightly above them. There were so many more layers of stars visible from the wide-open desert than she'd ever observed from the windows of the many homes and estates she'd grown up in. Homes and estates that her father had since liquidated, with the money disappearing from his coffers, drained to some ravenous void.

"My father used to be a very wealthy man. We had country homes, coastal homes, apartments in all the major cities…." She worked up the courage to look Alec in the eye. "From what I've been able to piece together since I learned what my father was doing, he began selling off these properties about eight years ago, liquidating all his assets until now, all they have left is their yacht."

Alec's eyes bored into hers. "Do you think your father helped finance the accident that caused my grandparents' helicopter wreck?"

"He financed *something*. That money is gone. I'm sure overturning a government is an expensive undertaking. They'd have to buy people's allegiance, their cooperation—"

"Their silence." Alec shook his head. "I was eighteen when my grandparents died suddenly, with little explanation. I asked my father why there wasn't a more extensive inquiry into what caused the accident. He never gave me a satisfactory answer."

Tears leaked down Lillian's cheeks at the thought of a teenage Alec mourning his grandparents' deaths, troubled by questions no one would answer. "I'm sorry."

"It's all right." A wry half smile bent the uninjured side of his face. "We can't go back in time and change what happened. But I want you to think about this..." His finger traced her cheek again, and for a moment she thought he might be about to kiss her again. Instead he finished, "I was going to try to get back to Sardis as soon as possible. But there may be a reason why God has led us to this place. We're in a unique position here. Knowing what we now know, I'm starting to think the best way I can help my family is by putting a stop to your uncle's plans."

The horses whinnied impatiently, but Alec's eyes never left her face.

Lily could feel her heart thumping hard as she considered the implications of his evolving strategy. "I'll do whatever I can to help you. I already offered to spy on them for you."

But Alec shook his head. "I don't want to push you into anything you might later regret doing."

"My uncle pulled a gun on me."

"You wouldn't just be opposing your uncle. Siding with me would mean opposing your own parents. I know you're upset with them, but they're your *parents*. I won't ask you to help me—"

"Alec, listen," she interrupted him, "I know you love and respect *your* parents, but my family isn't like yours. My entire childhood was one move after another, one nanny after another. I'd go days, even weeks at a time without seeing either of my folks, and they never seemed to care. I was a tool for them, a prop to be pulled out when having a child was expedient, and then they put me in storage like the rest of their toys when I wasn't useful anymore." In spite of her best efforts to remain indifferent as she recounted the events of her childhood, Lily heard an undercurrent of emotion cutting through her voice.

Alec must have heard it, too, because he reached for her again, wrapping her in the comfort of his embrace. "I'm sorry."

"You're not the one who needs to apologize. For years I thought if I was good enough I could earn their love. But as I grew older I questioned whether that was something I wanted to strive for, and over the course of the last couple of months, I've finally realized there's nothing to be gained by chasing their affection, because they're only going to betray me to get what they want."

Almost as though the horse sensed her emotional upheaval, the Arabian behind her extended her nose toward Lily's shoulder, nudging her in a reassuring way. Lily smiled at the animal's gesture, though it dredged up painful memories, as well.

Since Alec continued to hold her in silence, she gulped a breath and finished her story. "My father has been selling everything he owns. The last estate to go was the farm and the stable in upstate New York. My folks were living there, just two hours' drive away from where I was finishing my degree in veterinary medicine at Cornell, and Dad decided to let go of the stable hands. We had seventeen horses. My father didn't care about the horses. I don't know how he and my mother imagined they were going to take care of them alone, since neither of them can stand doing manual labor. He called me in April and announced he cancelled the contract with the vet we've always kept on retainer, and appointed me the official vet.

"I was studying for finals. I told him to hold off. I was so busy, I didn't have time to sleep, let alone drive down and make sure the horses were okay. Then he bought a load of alfalfa from a discount supplier down south, someone we've never worked with before. He got a great deal on the hay—that should have been a red flag right there. But instead of checking the hay or waiting for me, he fed it to the horses." Her voice caught. "To *all* the horses."

"It wasn't okay?"

Lillian shook her head, remembering. "It was riddled with blister beetles—which are poisonous to horses, absolutely deadly. When I got home and checked on it, I could see the beetles right there in the hay. But by then, it was too late. My father didn't call me at the first sign of a problem. He waited until after I'd graduated and was coming home. Three horses had already died. I did everything I could, but there was nothing more I could do." She swiped at her tears. "We lost them all."

"Why kill the horses?"

"Hmm?" Lillian tried not to let her emotions show, but the loss was still too fresh. She'd felt so helpless.

"If your father was selling everything else he owned, why not *sell* the horses? Why kill them?"

Lillian froze. She hadn't said that her father had killed the horses on purpose. She hadn't dreamed he would. But as she thought back over the events she'd just recounted, she saw how the soldier had reached that conclusion. "You think he killed them—deliberately?"

Alec shrugged, his muscular shoulders straining against his T-shirt as he moved. "Did he? I thought that's what you were telling me. Maybe it was an accident."

But Lillian's heart was already thumping hard with the realization. "No." She pinched her eyes shut, but her eyes felt dry, especially after so many days in the desert. "You're right. He didn't care if they were poisoned. They were heavily insured. He probably got more money from their deaths than he would have by selling them. It must have been the fastest way to liquidate them. He'd already sold off the estate—the new owners took possession a week after the last horse died." She shuddered, remembering how terrified she'd felt when she'd identified what was killing the horses, and realized she would likely be unable to save any of them.

"I can't believe your parents put you through that, especially knowing how much you love horses."

"That's just how they do things." Lily inhaled deeply, wishing she could clear the memories from her mind as easily as drawing in a fresh breath. "My point in telling you this is that I don't owe them anything, certainly not my allegiance. But they are my parents." A slight smile pulled at the corners of her mouth.

"What are you saying?"

"You need to find out what they're up to if you're going to put a stop to their plans to take over Lydia. It would be helpful to have someone on the inside, someone who could gather information for you."

Alec's arms tightened around her. "I won't let you endanger yourself."

"We're both already in danger. No one in your family will be safe until my uncle has been stopped. If I can expedite his capture…"

"If he finds out what you're up to—"

"That's a chance I'm willing to take." She grabbed the halter of her horse, preparing to climb on again. "We need to get moving while it's still dark. We can discuss our plans on the way."

"Let's go, then. But I won't knowingly allow you to endanger yourself." Alec helped her onto her horse and kissed her hand. "You mean too much to me."

In spite of her reservations about what they might find ahead of them, Lily smiled at his gesture as Alec climbed onto the gelding and led them northward again.

Alec kept his eyes on the stars, their only compass in a sea of sand. He reminded himself that it was only Monday morning. Lillian's parents would have to make excellent time sailing their yacht to have arrived at David's pier already. More likely they'd make port some time that afternoon, assuming they were headed that direction at all.

One thing was certain: he wasn't about to let Lillian inside her uncle's compound until her parents arrived there. Granted, it didn't sound as though her parents were very protective of her, but if their strongest motivation was selfishness, they'd keep Lily relatively safe because of her connection to them. From what he'd seen of her uncle David, he wasn't nearly so cautious.

As they traveled north toward the Mediterranean coast, the empty sand became pocked with sparse bushes and rocks, which grew thicker the farther they traveled. By morning, the ground was littered with scrubby grass, and the landscape edged with rugged boulders.

They stopped to drink shortly after the sun rose, and Alec surveyed the surrounding landscape through the binoculars he'd bought from the Bedouin merchant.

"See anything?" Lily asked as she replaced the cap on a canteen.

"Your uncle's compound is visible to the north. We've got to be within twenty kilometers, maybe less. We'll have to find cover before we go much farther, or his sentries will spot us. And we need to find a place to leave the horses before we proceed on foot."

Lily nodded solemnly. "What about water? We're running low."

"We'll come up with something." Alec replaced the binoculars in their case. "From here, I think we should veer toward the east. The vegetation looks denser in that direction."

"Trees have to have water, right?"

"Somewhere."

By midmorning the desert heat slowed their steps, and Alec was relieved to find a narrow ravine northward, becoming a deeper chasm as it spread toward the sea.

"I suspect your uncle's port is somewhere near the head of this," Alec observed. "We'll proceed cautiously. General Bardici chose the location of his fortress strategically. He's on the highest point along the coastline. There isn't anywhere we can go to look down on him."

"But he can look down on us." Lily peered up the sides of the ravine as if expecting to see soldiers staring down at them from the edge.

Alec found a patch of grass in the shade of the canyon cliffs. "Let's tie the horses here for now. I'm going to take a look ahead of us on foot."

"Mind if I come with you?"

"Don't you want to rest?"

"I'm tired, but I don't think I'll be able to sleep until I know where we stand."

Alec felt the same way. Together they continued down the rocky ravine, occasionally climbing the western ridge to get a look in the direction of the looming fortress. Finally, they reached a spot from which they could see her uncle's port.

"No sign of your parents' boat." Alec observed through the binoculars, scouring what he could of the sea to make sure the yacht wasn't approaching.

"Hopefully they'll be along today. In the meantime, we need to rest before we make any sort of move. Let's get back to the horses."

As they retraced their steps, Alec kept his eyes open for any sign of water. A leafy vine trailing down the far canyon wall caught his eye, and he trotted over to where it grew, peeling back the leaves to reveal a trickle of water that pooled in the vegetation-covered sand below.

He shoveled back sand with his hands, forming a depression deep enough to scoop water from. "It's fresh," he said, tasting it to be certain the seawater to the north hadn't contaminated it. "We can get the horses and bring them here. This will be a good spot to camp for the day."

"But it's on the east side of the ravine. If my uncle's men look over the west side, they'll spot us right away."

Alec couldn't deny the risk. "We can only pray they aren't looking for us this close to the compound. And we'll camp under the western lip of rock, just across from the water." He wished there was a safer place to hide, but they needed to stay close to a water supply. "It's the best option I've seen."

"You're right." Lily drank from the tiny pool. "Okay, let's grab the horses so we can get some rest. I'm dead on my feet, and I'm sure you're even more exhausted, since you didn't get any sleep yesterday."

Alec didn't deny her assessment, but in some ways, he was glad to be so tired. If he hadn't been so fatigued, he was certain he wouldn't be able to sleep for worrying over his concerns for their safety, the safety of his family members, and all of Lydia.

When Lily next opened her eyes, she saw that night had fallen. Instantly alert, she sat up and found Alec snoozing on the other side of the horses, his handsome face looking weary in the moonlight, the scars from the attack in Sardis healing over, obscured by the stubble of three days' worth of beard.

The horses slept as well, no doubt glad for the shade and relatively plentiful supply of grass in the wadi. Moving silently back toward the place where she'd slept, she settled in again, but this time, sleep evaded her. She had too much on her mind.

The brief glimpse she'd gotten of her uncle's compound the day before had sent fear rocketing straight to her heart. Was she crazy for volunteering to face her uncle again? Memories of the rough way he'd handled her the last time ricocheted through her mind, and she felt the tender spot under her jaw where he'd rammed his gun.

Her uncle had to be stopped. Ever since she and

Alec had pieced together the family connection, she'd become increasingly convinced her uncle planned to take over the Lydian government—and might already be well on his way to overtaking it, for all she knew.

Going inside his compound was the best way she could think of to gain information about what he was up to. If she could pass what she learned on to Alec, maybe they could put her uncle's plans to an end. But the thought of leaving Alec behind in the desert tore at her heart. She felt safe when she was with him. Safe and, for the first time she could remember, loved.

Her heart pinched at the thought of leaving him. Would they ever be reunited? Even if they managed to thwart her uncle's plans and return Alec's family to their rightful throne, surely Alec wouldn't want her around after that. Surely he'd want to rid himself of any reminder of the Bardici family, after all the trouble her uncle had caused him.

As emotion welled in her dry throat, Lily decided she needed a drink, and headed in the direction of the trickling waterfall.

No sooner had she finished drinking than she heard a distinct sound behind her, the all-too-familiar sound of a cocking gun.

"Don't move." It was Alec's voice.

Lillian froze.

Was Alec pointing a gun at her?

ELEVEN

A blast struck the ground only a couple of feet to her left, and Lily let out a quick scream as she leapt back.

Alec's arms wrapped around her instantly. "I got him. You're safe now."

Confused, Lily looked at the splattered spot where Alec's bullet had hit the sand, and saw the twitching tail of a snake writhing in the darkness.

"Cobra." Alec identified the deceased reptile. "The distance they can strike is equal to the height of their head above the ground."

"He could have bitten me?"

"Still could, even dead." Alec's protective grasp tightened around her. "I didn't see which way the head flew."

Lily clung to him and whimpered. "I didn't even see him."

"They like to hang out under rocks, in the shade. They're not usually active at night, but the sun just went down a little while ago, so it's still warm out.

He was probably just coming home for the night when he saw you stealing his water. Didn't look too happy about it."

"How did you see him?"

"I'm trained to spot these things. I saw you head for the water and thought maybe I should follow you."

"I'm glad you did." Cautiously they picked their way back toward the sleeping horses. "And I'm glad you brought your gun. Is that the one you got from the Bedouins who attacked you?"

"Yes. I also took his phone, but I turned it off right away to conserve the battery. Now that we've found water and we're settled in to camp, I thought I might use the satellite internet access to learn what I can about the situation in Lydia."

"Mind if I read over your shoulder?"

He still had his arms around her, and pulled her close. "Please do."

The affection in his voice sent a ripple of warmth through her, chasing away the cold fear she'd felt when she'd realized how close she'd come to being bitten by the poisonous snake. Once again, Alec had protected her. How would she get along inside her uncle's compound without him?

Alec powered the phone on, relieved to see it still had plenty of battery life remaining, and quickly found articles relating to the events in

Lydia. His sister Isabelle had escaped the attacks, traveled to New York City and spent the day meeting with the United Nations, who'd dispatched a team to Lydia following her testimony.

"Good job, Isabelle." He cheered his sister on when he read what she'd been up to. God had been with her—and perhaps she could make inroads toward restoring the Royal House of Lydia to the throne. But he couldn't help wondering what had become of the rest of his family. He scrolled through the search results again. "There's no word on Anastasia or my parents. But it does note that the American ambassador, Stephanos Valli, has stepped down from his post."

"Valli?" Lily stiffened behind him, and Alec recalled her earlier mention of the name.

"Your grandmother Helen—" he began.

"Valli was her first husband's last name," Lily confirmed. "Stephanos Valli is my half uncle, her only son from her first marriage."

"What kind of relationship does he have with your father?"

"They never used to get along, but while we were docked in Lydia, Uncle Steve called a few times."

"Did you visit him while you were in Sardis?"

"No, but he came to Uncle Dave's house one night, and the three brothers were up all night talking."

"Plotting?"

"I suppose so." Lily deflated. "Why didn't I think to listen in on what they were talking about? I could have heard something. I might have found out what was going on."

"And then what? You'd have only left town sooner, and then I never would have met you." Alec turned until he faced her where she sat reading over his shoulder.

She pulled back.

He leaned closer. "Don't blame yourself for not knowing. You couldn't have known. No one knew—in fact, from what I can gather from these articles, no one knows about your father and uncle's involvement. My sister uncovered Valli's plots, but even if she suspected the connection with your uncle, I doubt anyone knows where to find him. I've been serving in North Africa under Bardici's command, and had no idea he had a fortress on this side of the desert."

Lily's mouth set in a determined line. "That's all the more reason why I have to get inside his compound. Alec, we're the only ones who know he's out here. We can bring him down."

Alec's heart thumped out a fear-filled plea for her safety. "The more I think about you going in there, the less I like the idea. The place is crawling with soldiers."

"They're Lydian soldiers though, right? You've served alongside them, haven't you?"

"Yes, but they answer to your uncle, not to me. I may be heir to the throne, but I'm only a lieutenant in the Lydian army." He shook his head. "Besides, you escaped into the desert with me three days ago. They're sure to have received the picture the Bedouin texted to them yesterday, so they know I'm alive. They'll know we were together. If you walk in there, what are you going to tell them? They're going to demand to know where I am. If they dispatch soldiers to check the immediate area it will only be a matter of time before I'm found."

"What then?" Lillian's expression hardened. "We'll just stay hiding here in the ravine until we die of hunger or we're *both* captured? The only way to help your family is by stopping my uncle."

"I agree with that, I just don't think—"

"You don't think I can handle it?"

"It's too dangerous, Lillian." He heard his voice rising, but he didn't care. She had to understand.

"It's not as though I'd be any safer *not* going in."

Alec felt his hands tighten to fists, but there was nothing for him to attack, no present enemy for him to strike. A zealous desire to protect Lily rose up inside him, but there was nothing he could do to defend her. "I'm the trained soldier. I'm the one who should be dispatched on a mission. You're an innocent civilian."

"I'm not innocent. I'm a Bardici. My family is treasonous, and if I don't stand up to them, you might as well put me on trial alongside them once they're all captured."

"*If* they're captured. If they win—"

"We can't let them win."

"Aah." Alec let out a growl of frustration and looked up at the starlit desert sky. He couldn't stand the thought of Lily facing her murderous uncle. The very idea made him want to wrap his arms around her and shield her from anything and everything that could ever hurt her. She'd already paid far too high a price for her father's ambition. All she'd wanted was her parents' love, or the companionship of the animals she'd tried to rescue, but her parents had withheld their affection and killed off her horses. "It's not fair."

"What isn't?"

"That you should have to face them again. You've already risked your life. You've already paid too high a price."

Hope crept onto Lily's face. "You're thinking of letting me go in."

"I don't like it, but I don't see any way around it."

Lily nodded. "At first light tomorrow I'll take an empty canteen and walk up to the door of my uncle's fortress. I'll tell him I took your water while you were sleeping and left you for dead in the desert." She grinned mischievously. "It's more or less true."

Alec felt the corners of his mouth bend upward at the sight of her smile. "You're not going in until your parents have arrived. And we'll have to work out some way for you to communicate with me." He looked down at the phone in his hands, and powered it off. "I'll need to save the battery."

"Fair enough." Her smile looked tired, but still hope-filled. "It will come out all right."

"Will it?" Alec pulled her close, wrapping his arms around her and wishing he didn't have to let her go. But she was right—there wasn't any other way out of their situation than to face their troubles head-on and defeat them—even if that meant defeating her family.

His thoughts churned as he held her tight against him. His goals had changed. He wasn't just fighting for the safety of his family and the freedom of Lydia anymore. No, somehow, once his family was safe and Lydia's freedom had been insured, he was going to give Lily all that her family had taken from her: her freedom and unconditional love.

Lily clutched the empty canteen as she made her way across the desert sand, glad she hadn't waited for the sun to rise completely before starting the trek to her uncle's front door. Already heat had begun to rise in the desert. Combined with the cold terror inside her, it made her feel sick to her stomach.

She reminded herself that her parents' yacht had docked near the compound sometime during the night. From what she'd seen of it through Alec's binoculars, her parents had already gone to see her uncle. Anyway, the yacht was being guarded by armed soldiers, and she was glad Alec had agreed with her not to try to take the boat. Her uncle's helicopter would catch up to them before they made it out to sea, and then they'd only be in that much more trouble.

No, she knew her current strategy was the only plan that had any chance at all of working. Prayers accompanied each step as she made her way through the sand.

Tears sprang to her eyes, and she clutched the canteen a little more tightly. Even when she felt as though she didn't have the strength to go on, she wasn't alone. God was with her. He'd seen her through the last three days, and when she'd been too exhausted to move, God had used Alec to carry her over the ridges of sand.

God had provided. And in the middle of the desert, when everything had seemed beyond hope, God had given her a special gift: the affection of a prince.

She'd always longed for love. Alec's affection was more than she'd hoped for, and she wasn't going to let him down now. He had every reason to hate her for what her family had done to his.

No, the only way she could make things right between them was by bringing her traiterous uncle to justice, and learning the truth about her parents' involvement.

Looking up, she saw the front gates of her uncle's compound open, and three horsemen poured through. Her heart beat hard. She wouldn't have to knock on the doors after all. They'd seen her approaching, and they were coming for her.

"Watch over me," she whispered to God as the horsemen drew quickly closer. She raised her head to meet them. She had a mission to accomplish. After all, how could she possibly face Alec again unless she faced the demons in her family?

Alec trained his binoculars on the compound, dodging the scraggly branches of the tall bushes that provided his meager cover, shielding the instrument with his hands to keep the field glasses from reflecting the sun's light and drawing attention to his hiding place.

Granted, the men who'd ridden out to meet Lily seemed to be focused on her, but that didn't mean there weren't sentries scouring the surrounding countryside for him already.

Bless her heart, Lily had insisted on taking a circuitous route to keep the men from following her footsteps back to their campground. She'd found the rockiest patches of desert to clamber across, obscuring even the faintest traces of her footprints. What little she'd left behind was already being filled in by the skittering sands driven by the desert breeze.

His location was more or less secure. Lily was the one taking all the risks, and he kept up a continual prayer for her safety. "Grant her courage, Lord. Grant her a room with an outside view."

Lily would need a window, preferably a window overlooking the desert, and not the inner courtyard of the compound. They'd arranged a signal. If it was safe for him to approach, she'd tie her window curtains in a knot through the window. That way, he'd know which room she was in, and he'd only be alerted if she had information to pass along to him.

And if she wasn't able to learn anything that would help him, she'd keep her head down and her window shades closed. Neither of them wanted to risk anything unless there was something to be gained.

For now, it was enough to see that the men who escorted her into the compound appeared to be handling her gently. One even got off his horse so she could ride while he walked alongside. It was a good sign, and it boded well for his hopes that her family would receive her, if not with open arms, at least without chaining her up somewhere. She'd need her freedom if she was going to learn anything more about the plot against the Lydian kingdom.

Lily felt a rising sense of impatience. In the day and a half she'd been inside her uncle's compound, she'd had five good meals, several snacks, two showers and a bath. Her parents had even accompanied her to the yacht, where she'd claimed her own clothes and shoes, as well as the Bible from her bedside nightstand.

Now she turned the pages of the good book impatiently, reading the promises God had given his people in the generations past, saving them from their enemies, reclaiming them when foreign nations had carried them off in exile. She read God's promises in the book of Isaiah, and smiled at the words of Isaiah 30:21.

Whether you turn to the right or to the left, your ears will hear a voice behind you, saying, "This is the way; walk in it." She prayed God would guide her, that God would be with her as He had been with His people throughout history.

The words echoed with a timeless truth. God had been faithful to His people, even when they hadn't been faithful to Him. It only seemed right, then, that God should help the Royal House of Lydia reclaim the crown that was rightfully theirs. After all, they had never turned their backs on Him.

But other than catching up on her Bible reading, Lily hadn't learned a thing. She hadn't even seen her uncle, and her parents had talked to her as though nothing had happened, telling her all about the fish her father had caught the day after she'd left them—as though she'd no more than gone to visit a friend for a few days, and missed all the fun.

She didn't dare ask any direct questions for fear of rousing their suspicions. After all, she'd never cared about politics before. She figured she should be grateful they'd believed her story about leaving Alec for dead in the desert, barely escaping the desert heat with her life. Though a team of horsemen had gone out to the south, from what Lily had seen of their journey, they hadn't ventured eastward to where Alec was actually hiding.

He was safe.

For now.

But in the meantime, the hours were ticking by like sand through an hourglass. Her uncle still roamed far too freely. Something had to happen soon. "Lord, please help me. I need a break. I need a clue—something. You know what rests in the balance. And be with Alec. Protect him Lord, please."

She bent her head over the Bible, repeating her heartfelt prayer, when a knock sounded at the door to her suite.

She leapt up to answer it, surprised to see her uncle David and her father on the other side.

Her uncle spoke. "We have something to discuss with you. Would you please come with us?"

Lily didn't hesitate. After all, the last time she'd resisted her uncle, he'd put a gun to her neck. This time he'd actually said *please*.

It didn't bode well.

Her heart hammered hard inside her as the two men led her down the stairs from her second-floor suite, past the elaborate main-floor landing, to a second set of stairs that twisted past a steel door and disappeared into darkness underground.

David Bardici hit a switch, and artificial light illuminated the gray-painted cement steps. Unlike the rich decor aboveground, there was nothing pretty about where they were going, but Lily followed, praying silently that somehow God would use whatever was about to happen to help Alec's family.

They came to a large office, where an open table occupied the center of the drab room, and computers on desks lined the back cinder-block wall. Lily wished she could go online and read the news about the situation in Lydia, but her uncle motioned for her to sit in the lone chair facing away from the computers, while he and her father took the chairs on the opposite side of the table.

She braced herself for questions. Would they

ask for more information about Alec? Steeling herself against giving away her feelings for the prince, she was surprised when her uncle didn't even mention him.

"As you may know, the kingdom of Lydia is in turmoil. The king has been missing for five days, and Parliament cannot do any official business without the consent of the crown."

Lily hadn't realized the part about Parliament, only that Isabelle had met with them. She raised a curious eyebrow as her uncle continued.

"What you may not realize is that our family is descended from the Lydian monarchy. In the king's absence, we've asked that Parliament revisit the Articles of Succession. At this point, it remains unclear who the rightful rulers of Lydia should be. Your father and I are certain we will soon be vindicated in our claim to the crown, but until then, Parliament is drafting a proposed compromise."

Surprise lifted Lily's other eyebrow. She couldn't see how Parliament could possibly choose her family over Alec's, especially after the nefarious things her uncle had done to unseat the Royal House of Lydia. Unless they didn't know what her uncle had been up to...

"Only a member of the Royal House of Lydia can be crowned," her uncle continued. "We are members of that family, and the crown was stolen from us nearly a century ago. Until we can prove to Parliament that King Philip's family has no right to rule, we must compromise with them and form an oligarchy, a ruling partnership made up of all contenders to the throne."

Her father cleared his throat. "It will fulfill all the political requirements. Only those eligible to rule will be included, but no one family will be given power over the other."

Lily's heart pounded hard inside her. She'd wondered why they'd been treating her so well since her return. Now everything began to make sense. They needed her. Recalling the family tree Alec had etched in the desert sand, she realized there were only a handful of biological descendants of Lydia. Alec's father and siblings were the progeny of Alexander, while her father and uncles were the offspring of Alexander's older half brother, Basil. With her half uncle Stephanos Valli removed from his position in disgrace, her father and uncle needed her more than ever.

Once again, it was expedient for her selfish family to have a daughter, to have a puppet they could pull out for show, before she wasn't needed and they cast her aside again.

"We need you," her uncle concurred, "to travel with us to Sardis as soon as Parliament announces a decision. There will be a document to be signed. The three of us are all eligible to represent our family. Philip's family only has one representative, Princess Isabelle."

Michael cleared his throat. "We've heard that Anastasia…"

David nodded. "Anastasia may also potentially sign the document. That is why we must have your support to have a majority."

Lily pinched her lips shut. Isabelle and Anastasia weren't the only siblings. There was the missing oldest brother, Thaddeus, who was as yet unaccounted for, and of course, King Philip himself. And Alec. If her father or uncle knew that Alec had survived, they might try to have him killed to keep him from upsetting their majority in the oligarchy.

"So, Lillian." David stood. "You are prepared to sign whatever we place in front of you in Sardis." It wasn't a question.

She looked up at her uncle, his stern face expecting compliance, his fingers resting on the handle of the gun that protruded from the holster at his hip.

More than her uncle's threat of violence, her hopes of discovering information that could help Alec led her to comply. There was absolutely nothing to be gained by resisting her uncle. Her only option was to gain their trust enough to learn more about what they were up to. "I'll do whatever you ask me to."

"Excellent." His smile twisted her stomach in knots. "Come with me."

With only a brief glance at the computers she would so have loved to use, Lily followed her uncle and father back upstairs to her room, where they left her inside and closed the door with an extra click.

She checked the knob a moment later.

Locked.

So, then, that was it. She wasn't sure why they'd taken her downstairs, but could only assume they suspected she might have resisted them.

One other thing was certain. If they were traveling back to Sardis as soon as Parliament made an announcement, she didn't have time to waste. Alec would have to be warned immediately. He needed to get back to Sardis, though she couldn't imagine how he would get there in time. Hopeless tears coursed down her cheeks, but then her gaze fell on the open Bible she'd left behind.

God rescued His faithful people.

"Help me to be more faithful, Lord," she whispered. "I can't do this without You."

Alec trained his binoculars on the Bardici compound. The swirling in his empty stomach only reinforced his growing fears. Lily had been inside the estate for over thirty-eight hours. In that time, he'd seen a female figure standing in a window looking out, but no curtains had been knotted. No signal had been given. Why not?

He'd dared to turn on the Bedouin's phone to check the internet briefly that afternoon, but other than a rumor about a possible compromise between the Bardici family and his, there was no news out of Lydia.

Something had to give soon. His stores of food were gone, and he'd been living off of water from the tiny trickle in the ravine. Even the horses had consumed most of the grass in the immediate area. Besides running out of options, there was every chance they might be discovered at any time.

As the sun dipped low in the western sky, Alec focused his field glasses on the window where he'd spotted the female figure the day before. A shadow passed across the curtain.

Movement.

Someone was there.

He adjusted the resolution, though no amount of focus could compel the figure to appear again.

Then the curtains shifted, stirred up by someone inside. The window latch opened and a swath of something sage-green fluttered in the open air.

The window shut, but the sage-green bulge remained, a knot in the window curtain.

Lily's signal.

It was time. She had a message for him. And, for the moment at least, the coast was clear.

* * *

Lily fluffed her hair and popped another mint into her mouth, chastising her reflection in the mirror. "He doesn't care what you look like," she told herself.

But she didn't believe it. Inconsequential as her appearance might be under the circumstances, she still wanted to look her best when she saw Alec again. After all, he was a prince. Even though she'd told herself a thousand times over that whatever was between them would undoubtedly end once their ordeal was over, she couldn't help the way her heart beat excitedly at the thought of seeing him again.

She crossed to the window and peered out into the darkness. Was he even out there? Had he come up with a different plan and left the desert behind? Had he been captured while approaching? Anything could happen to him.

A canteen landed with a clunk on the tiny balcony outside her window. Lily opened the casement and grabbed the canteen, turning it over to reveal a note.

TIE ME UP.

Lily blinked at the handwritten letters, then quickly guessed at what Alec was up to. A long rope extended from the sand-filled canteen, and she twined it around the balusters, knotting it tightly over the top of the railing.

A moment later there was a tug on the rope, and she looked down to see Alec climbing up.

Her heart leapt at the sight of him, and she wanted to call down to him to be careful, but at the same time, she couldn't risk doing anything that might give away his presence.

His hands gripped the railing, and an instant later he'd hoisted himself over it.

She pulled him back into her suite, and he stumbled after her, wrapping his arms around her and pressing his face close to hers.

She hadn't had any intention of kissing him, but the moment his lips drew near, she didn't hesitate to return his eager kiss.

"Are you all right? They haven't hurt you?" he whispered between kisses.

"I'm fine, but you've got to get to Sardis as soon as you can. There's going to be a ruling oligarchy. You've got to sign it or our family will outnumber yours."

"Outnumber?"

"My uncle and father and I make three. Your two sisters are only two."

"You'd sign—" Alec began, and for the first time stopped kissing her.

"I've got to go along with what they ask. If I don't—"

Before she could finish her sentence, the lights snapped on. The door to her suite was open, and her room was filled with soldiers, surrounding them with their guns trained on them from every angle.

David Bardici smiled. "Good work, Lillian. Your cooperation is very much appreciated." He nodded to the armed men. "Handcuff him. Let's go."

Lily blinked against the sudden light, unsure how or when the men had entered her room. Her entire attention had been so focused on Alec, she'd been unaware of anything else.

But he didn't know that.

As soldiers clapped cuffs on Alec's wrists, he looked at her with disappointment in his eyes, and she realized with a stab of horror how the situation looked from his perspective.

He thought she'd worked with her uncle to purposely trap him, didn't he?

And she had no way of proving to him otherwise.

TWELVE

Alec strained against the chains that bound him, but they didn't budge.

He knew there was no point fighting, but he couldn't help it. He had to do something. He'd been so foolish.

With his kingdom and the lives of his family hanging in the balance, he'd walked right into a trap. Could he have been any more stupid?

Good work, Lillian. Your cooperation is very much appreciated.

David Bardici's words echoed through his mind, at odds with the expression on Lily's face. She'd looked startled. Horrified. Desperate.

Had she betrayed him? He didn't want to believe it, but the chains on his wrists said otherwise.

Whatever her role had been, he had only himself to blame for getting captured. Why had he thought he could walk into Bardici's compound and emerge unharmed? More importantly, why had he given in to his longing to hold Lillian in his arms and kiss her again, allowing himself to be distracted instead of realizing the danger in time to escape? He'd told himself a hundred times as he'd prepared for his visit that it was a fact-finding mission only. He'd had no intention of kissing her.

But the moment he saw her, there had been no resisting the pull of attraction he felt. He'd been so concerned for her safety, so worried that she might be suffering at the hands of her evil uncle.

Now he was going to suffer at her uncle's hands. It was only a matter of time.

With a reverberating boom, a door opened, and several sets of feet shuffled through the darkness.

"When your family is hanged for treason and my family takes the throne, don't blame *me,* Alexander." David Bardici's voice carried through the cavernous space. "Blame yourself. You failed them. You failed God." He chuckled.

Alec's hands clenched, but there was nothing he could do to defend himself.

"Don't worry about Lillian's safety anymore. She did exactly what we asked her to do from the very beginning. She found you during the ambush. She seduced you. She fooled you into thinking she could be trusted and then she betrayed you. As long as she continues to cooperate with us, she will be rewarded handsomely for her work. But if you attempt to contact her, if you ever try to see her again, we'll hang her right beside you. Understand?"

Alec said nothing, and a hollow boom told him the general had left.

In his absence, Alec wrestled with the man's question. Did he understand?

Maybe.

If Lillian really was cooperating with her uncle, would the general have had to warn him away from her?

There was an undercurrent of fear that carried through the man's threat, a needlessness that could only be explained one way.

David Bardici knew that Alec was in love with his niece. And he didn't want Alec getting close to her again. Why not?

Was Lillian's love for him stronger than her fear of her uncle?

Alec prayed he'd somehow get the chance to find out.

Lillian followed her uncle silently as he shoved her from the dark room, the words he'd used to taunt Alec still ringing in her ears.

If you attempt to contact her, if you ever try to see her again, we'll hang her right beside you. She knew the warning was as much for her benefit as for his. Wasn't that why her uncle had dragged her down to the dungeon to hear him threaten Alec in the first place?

She told herself he was being a bully, but that knowledge brought her little comfort in the face of the overwhelming reality. David Bardici had made Alec believe that every kindness Lily had shown him since the moment they'd met in the alley had only been to earn his trust so she could lead him into their trap. Worse than that, she was certain her uncle had every intention of killing Alec once he was certain he had no need of him. And once he no longer had any need of her?

He'd put her away for good this time.

"Through here." David shoved her into the same office he'd taken her to earlier that day, planting her in the chair opposite his while he picked up one of the computers from the desk along the wall and plunked it down in front of her. Though it looked like any ordinary computer, several cords dangled from it, and he pulled a few more gadgets from a case. "Now that I've taken care of that, I have an assignment for you. Give me your arm."

"Is that really necessary?" Michael Bardici had followed them silently until now.

"Don't question me." David barked at his little brother without taking his eyes off Lily. "Your arm."

Lillian reluctantly lifted the requested append-age, and her uncle put a blood-pressure cuff on her, followed by another smaller cuff for her finger. Then he plucked two unfamiliar cables from the case.

"Respiration transducers," he explained as he clipped them to the front of her shirt and plugged the other end into the computer. "It's a polygraph test."

"A lie detector?"

Her uncle ignored her question and scowled at the computer screen. "You are a nervous one, aren't you?" He clicked a few keys. "State your name."

"Lillian Bardici."

His face didn't leave the screen. "And you're in love with Prince Alexander, correct?"

In spite of anything she might have done to stop it, she felt her heart rate pick up and a blush rise straight to her cheeks.

Her uncle shook his head at her. "Really, Lillian, that's pathetic." He rolled his eyes and returned his attention to the screen. "At least you make my job easier. Now, has the prince been in contact with any other members of the royal family since the ambush?"

Lily didn't figure there would be any point in trying to lie. "Not that I'm aware of."

"Has he spoken to you about his brother?"

"Thaddeus?"

"He's spoken of him, then?"

"Just to say that he went out on a boat with a friend six years ago, and never came back."

"Is that all he said?"

"And that you want to know where he is."

Her uncle's eyes narrowed, and he turned his attention from the screen to her face. "He told you that I want to know where his brother is?"

She nodded.

"What exactly did he say?"

Lily tried to recall Alec's words, but her uncle's intimidating presence made thinking difficult. "You called him into your office in Benghazi and asked him if he knew where his brother was."

"He remembers." The general appeared to be upset by that revelation. It fit with Alec's fears that her uncle had used memory-erasing drugs on him. Obviously her uncle hadn't expected Alec to regain those hidden memories—but then he probably hadn't expected him to get amnesia during the motorcade ambush, either. "Does he know where his brother is?"

"No."

"Does he know what happened to his brother?"

Lily could feel her heart hammering in response to the question. She could only imagine what kind of answers her uncle was gleaning before she said a word.

"Tell me what you know," David Bardici demanded.

"Thaddeus went sailing. He never came back."

"What does Alexander believe happened to his brother?"

"He doesn't know."

Her uncle turned to her. "You know more than you're saying."

Lily took a deep breath and tried to think. She'd long ago given up any hope of misleading her uncle. Mostly she just wanted to placate his constant demands. "Thaddeus had a friend who was accused of killing him—Kirk." She pinched her eyes shut as she recalled the name. "Alec doesn't think Kirk did it. He doesn't think Kirk killed Thaddeus, or that he lied about it."

"Where does he think his brother went?"

"He doesn't know."

The general let out a frustrated breath. "Fine." He pulled a picture from the sheaf of papers he'd carried into the room. "Do you recognize this?"

Lily looked at the picture—some sort of jeweled scepter, inlaid with amethysts, with a cross on top. There was no caption to identify the object, but it looked a little familiar.

"You *do* recognize it," her uncle surmised, apparently from the expression on her face since she hadn't said anything for the polygraph to declare true or false.

"I—I don't know. I think I've seen it in a book somewhere."

"Where?"

Lillian tried frantically to recall. "A long time ago? I don't know. Maybe not."

"It's the Scepter of Charlemagne," her uncle reported brusquely. "Has the prince mentioned it to you?"

"Charlemagne," Lillian whispered, and closed her eyes, trying to recall what Alec had said. "Charlemagne was the Holy Roman Emperor."

"I'm not looking for a history lesson!" the general shouted. "I want to know what the idiot said."

"David," Michael chided his brother, who looked as though he might do something violent at any moment.

"He didn't say anything about a scepter," Lily told her uncle flatly, and had to assume the polygraph backed her up, because she really *didn't* know any more than that. But her uncle certainly seemed to think the scepter was important. Lily wondered why he was so desperate for information about it.

"Fine. Do you intend to sign the covenant and support the Bardici claim to the throne?"

"Yes."

Whatever the computer screen showed when

she answered the question, he didn't approve, but leaned across the table toward her. "I'm watching you, Lillian." He plucked the transducers from her shirt and jerked the cuff from her arm. "If you want to survive this revolution, you'll do exactly as I say." Then he pulled her across the room, past her father, opening the door to reveal soldiers standing guard in the hall.

"Lock her in her room." He shoved her toward them. "And see that she doesn't get out!"

Lillian went straight to her window, but saw to her disappointment that the rope she'd tied to the balusters earlier was gone.

Not that she expected to get very far without Alec's help.

With her door locked, she didn't have any way of reaching him, if he was even still inside the compound. Instead she fell backward on the bed while the tears flowed freely down her cheeks. Did Alec think she'd betrayed him? Did he hate her?

For a moment, she let herself remember the way he'd wrapped his arms around her, kissing her as though she meant the world to him, too wrapped up in the love between them to pay attention to any possible threat that might be lurking in the dark room.

Lillian shuddered as she thought about the number of soldiers who'd entered without her realizing it. Had her uncle suspected what she was about to do? Had he been spying on her and watching her create the signal with the window curtain? Or had he simply acted quickly the instant a wary guard had caught sight of Alec scaling her wall?

However he'd pulled it off, Lillian figured it didn't matter anyway. Her uncle was king of this castle, and he ruled with an iron fist. If he got control of the entire kingdom of Lydia, there would be no end to the trouble he might cause. The man was cruel and ruthless.

She couldn't let him get away with his plans.

But how could she stop him?

No sound penetrated the dark chamber where Alec was chained. Had he been there an hour? A day? There'd been no sign of anyone, save General Bardici and his hostile warning. Alec hadn't had anything to eat or drink. Were they planning to leave him there to die?

A hollow echo reverberated through the still air, and Alec wondered what it meant. A door had opened somewhere, not far from him. The slightest shift in the air whispered past his skin.

Someone was coming.

A moment later the light switched on, and Alec saw that he was in a stone-walled room. A soldier stood opposite him with keys in his hands. A greenish bruise colored the left side of his face.

The soldier touched the bruise with his fingertips as he approached. "It's been almost a week since you hit me with a cast-iron floor lamp and gave me this bruise."

Alec braced himself, trying to judge how upset the soldier was about what had happened. At the same time, he recognized the man from basic training. "Titus." Putting the pieces together, Alec recalled that Titus was the name of the soldier who'd dropped the canteen near them in the desert. He'd never determined whether the canteen had been offered as a lifeline or a trap. "I'm sorry."

The soldier shrugged off his apology. "I've asked myself since then what I would have done had our roles been reversed."

Alec considered mentioning that if he'd meant to kill the soldier with the blow, the man wouldn't have been standing there to accuse him. He'd only been trying to get away.

The man took a step closer. "I'd have probably broken your neck. That way, I wouldn't have to worry about what would happen when you got up." He reached for him.

Alec shifted to the side, but with his hands and ankles chained to the wall, he had no way of defending himself.

Lillian boarded the helicopter obediently and was relieved when she was allowed to sit in a seat, instead of being shoved into the luggage compartment this time. But then this helicopter was much more comfortably equipped than the military craft she'd been transported in the week before. Their ride back to Sardis would be considerably more luxurious than the trip to the desert had been.

While her father and uncle sat toward the front discussing their plans in low tones, Lily sat opposite her mother and wondered what role Sandra Bardici had been playing in the unfolding events. Since the woman was only a member of the family by marriage, and not a descendent of Lydia, she wasn't eligible to sign the covenant that Parliament had prepared. If Lily had been asked to describe her mom, she'd have called her submissive. Quiet. Dutiful.

For most of her life, Lily had watched her mother follow her father around, doing whatever he asked her to do, going where he told her. Rarely did the woman question anything.

Lily looked up at her mother, who offered her a pinched smile.

"Did you want something to drink? A sandwich?"

"I'm fine." Lily was tempted to ask if her mother realized what was going on, if she cared about what they were up to, but even if her mother had wanted to say something, the Bardici brothers were right behind her. Besides, what was there to discuss? Parliament had given all eligible descendants of Lydia forty-eight hours to sign the covenant. If Alec didn't get to the Hall of Justice in Sardis before that narrow window closed, he'd be left out.

There was nothing she could do to help him now.

Alec stumbled over the chains that bound his legs as Titus led him toward the waiting helicopter. Unlike the military craft that had brought him to North Africa, this copter was a sleek corporate craft, a limousine of the sky. Through the windows, Alec caught sight of several figures seated inside. The Bardicis?

Rather than seat him in the same comfortable compartment the passengers rode in, Titus led him to the rear door, a cramped, low-ceilinged secondary compartment filled mostly with luggage.

Another soldier appeared behind them as they climbed in. "Bardici said to secure him to the retaining rail."

Alec glanced at the metal bar high on the sides of the compartment. If they looped his cuffs through the rail, he'd dangle uncomfortably for the length of the trip.

Titus shoved him inside as he addressed the soldier who followed him in. "Do you suppose Bardici is coming back here to check?"

"Not this time." The other soldier chuckled as he took a seat on the floor. "You gonna chain him to the retaining rail?"

Titus nodded to Alec to sit. "Not this time."

Lily caught the movement outside the window, and looked just in time to see two soldiers hauling a bound man onto the copter. In spite of her partially obstructed view, Lily knew the man well enough to recognize him in that momentary glimpse.

Alec.

So he was coming to Sardis, too. Her heart soared with the knowledge that he would be in the same city as the document that required his signature. More than that, she wasn't alone—he was with her, even if they were separated by the partitions within the helicopter.

But as quickly as that realization hit, it was followed by another. Her uncle had warned Alec away from her. The prince probably hated her for betraying him, and even if he realized that she'd been as much a victim of her uncle's plot as he had, that didn't erase the threats that hung over both of them if they so much as tried to speak to one another again.

A chill sense of foreboding washed over her.

Her uncle was bringing Alec to Sardis. That meant he must have plans for him.

And David Bardici's plans for Alec couldn't be good.

Alec eyed the two soldiers warily. Titus hadn't said anything more since he'd taken a seat on the floor of the helicopter without cuffing him to the wall. Alec's wrists and ankles were still bound, but at least he wasn't dangling from the low ceiling.

The other man, who Alec recognized as Julian, another of the men he'd served with in Benghazi, sat grimly by the door, anger written in his posture and his face. Was he upset about being scrunched in the cramped luggage compartment? Offended that Titus hadn't chained up the prisoner?

Or was he, like Alec, outraged by all that General Bardici had gotten away with of late?

When the rotors thrummed up enough lift to pull them from the ground, Titus leaned closer to Alec. "Do you know about the covenant Parliament has arranged? All those with a claim to the crown must sign it by midnight, or forfeit their claim."

Alec felt his heart sink. "I'd heard rumors something like that might happen. Have any signed?"

"Both of your sisters."

Alec felt a wave of relief wash over him. Isabelle and Anastasia had accomplished far more than he had in the week since their motorcade had been ambushed. He'd always been proud of them, but never more so than that moment. At the same time, he felt the sting of his own failure.

"That's why Bardici is taking his brother and niece to Sardis on this flight," Julian explained, "and why he won't let you out of his sight. He's going to sign the document, and he'll do everything in his power to make sure you don't sign it."

"I'm surprised he hasn't killed me yet."

The two soldiers exchanged glances. "You're still too valuable to him alive," Titus told him. "Apparently you know something..."

"Something he needs to know," Julian finished.

Reassured that he wasn't about to be assassinated, Alec asked the question that had been troubling him since the men had mentioned his sisters. "What about my parents? Isn't my father eligible to sign this covenant, too?"

Titus let out a heavy breath, and Julian shook his head.

"The covenant is being kept at the Hall of Justice in Sardis. Your sisters both managed to sign the document, but they were attacked.

"Attacked?" Alec immediately felt concern for their safety.

"They're fine. They got away when your father arrived—no one had seen him before this, no one knew where he was…" Julian shook his head again.

Alec looked back and forth between the men. "My father made it to the hall?"

"He was shot," Titus admitted. "I don't believe he was killed. From what I've heard he's in a coma."

"But he didn't sign the covenant?"

"No," Julian confirmed. "That much I've heard with certainty. And that's why—" he stretched out his long legs in the cramped space of the rear helicopter compartment "—Titus and I have both decided to pledge our support to you. For the last week, no one knew where our king was, or if he'd abandoned us to the rebels. But that fact that he took a bullet defending his nation and his daughters—"

Titus picked up where his fellow soldier's words had dropped off. "You're his heir. We've seen enough of the way Bardici works to know we don't want him as our king. You could have killed me with that floor lamp last week, but you didn't."

"I didn't recognize you," Alec explained quickly. "I didn't even know who I was until a few days ago. The ambush wiped out my memory."

"We'd surmised as much." Julian nodded. "Whether you knew who anyone was or not, you still acted with greater honor and integrity than our general. You have our support."

"But—" Titus raised a hand of caution "—we have no way of gauging the support of the rest of the men, especially those we'll encounter in Sardis. They've been trained to follow their general's orders, and we can only assume they'll continue to do so."

"We'll be outnumbered in Sardis," Julian assured them. "Bardici only kept a skeleton crew at his African compound in order to avoid detection. He'll have hundreds of men in Sardis, instead of dozens. And I can't name a single one of them who would directly defy orders. None of them know you're alive. Bardici has given us instructions to put a bag over your head when we disembark. I doubt he's going to let anyone on to the knowledge that the Lydian heir is back on Lydian soil. There won't be anyone on the ground we can trust."

Alec nodded solemnly. There was one individual he hoped he could trust, but he wasn't about to mention her to the men. They'd already watched Lily betray him once. He knew they'd lose all faith in him if he suggested they trust her again. But that didn't keep him from praying that God would keep Lily safe. Whether she could be trusted or not, he didn't want anything to happen to her. She'd already suffered enough.

Lily's hand shook as she signed the covenant that would allow her to rule Lydia along with her father, uncle and Alec's two sisters. Somehow the signature still came out legible, though she couldn't help feeling that in signing her name, she'd sealed off any possibility that Alec might ever forgive her for her association with her family.

After all, she'd promised him she'd spy on her uncle to undermine his evil plans. In signing her name, she only buttressed his plans. But she didn't see any way around it. If she was going to stay in her uncle's good graces, she *had* to sign. Besides, signing only made her a member of the oligarchy. That didn't mean she'd vote alongside her uncle in oligarchical rulings. In fact, if she ever managed to wriggle out from under her uncle's thumb, she had every intention of using her newly claimed power to help Alec's family.

Of course, she couldn't let on about any of that to her uncle.

The general had already signed the covenant that morning, unwilling for the three of them to arrive at the Hall of Justice together, especially not after the violence that had met the princesses when they'd arrived to sign. But other than taking separate trips to the Hall of Justice, he hadn't let her or her father out of his sight.

Lily and her father climbed into the limousine, and she watched her father warily. This was the man who'd tossed Alec overboard, who'd called

David to come pluck them from the yacht, who'd ordered the hay that had poisoned her beloved horses.

Michael Bardici shook his head sadly. "You didn't want to sign it," he whispered from the seat beside her.

Lily shrugged. "I didn't have any choice, did I? Whether I run away or whether I comply, David gets his way."

"David always gets his way," her father repeated softly, and leaned closer to her, dropping his voice so she had to strain to hear. "And I'm getting tired of it. I shouldn't have let him take you from the yacht. I shouldn't have let him control me for so long."

Lily pulled back and studied her father's face. His warm brown eyes glimmered with regret, and his mouth was drawn in a thin frown.

"Alexander's family's claim to the throne rests on your great-grandfather's abdication," Michael Bardici explained. "If they could prove that Basil abdicated, David would have no further stake in the crown."

"Can they prove it?"

Her father shook his head. "Your uncle isn't working alone. He and the other Lydian generals are all on the payroll of a man who goes only by number 8. Six years ago, this 8 asked King Philip to verify Basil's abdication, and King Philip produced the abdication document."

Lily gasped. "So it really ex—"

Her father shushed her. Already their car had left the city and drew closer to David Bardici's country estate. They didn't have much longer to talk. "It *did* exist. 8 stole it. I had assumed the document was destroyed, but this is not the case. Earlier today when I opened your uncle's desk drawer for a pen, my fingers slipped on the release to a false drawer bottom. The abdication document is hidden in the false compartment. I caught only a glimpse of it before I shut the drawer for fear your uncle would see. Now I'm afraid he may suspect what I saw, because he won't let me out of his sight within the house."

"If I could get it—" Lily breathed, hope hammering against her heart as the car cleared the gates of the Bardici estate.

Her father shook his head. "You would have to be very careful, and even then, I don't know how you'd get it back to the royal family. But you have done many things in the past week I didn't know you were capable of. Perhaps…"

His sentence hung unfinished as the car came to a stop and her uncle waited for them to exit. And then, just as her father had intimated, David Bardici followed them both into the house, trailing her father as though he didn't dare let his eyes off him for one moment.

Lily's mother met her by the stairs and escorted her to her room. "Everything went smoothly?" Sandra Bardici confirmed.

"Without a hitch." Lily nodded. "Now I think I might rest."

Lily lingered in the doorway to her suite as her mother disappeared down the hall. Had her father told her the truth? Did the abdication document still exist, and was it even now inside the very estate where she was staying?

It almost seemed too good to be true—which was why she couldn't help wondering if her father's words were just another trap.

THIRTEEN

Lily stepped into the hall. They hadn't locked her in her room. Perhaps now that she'd signed the covenant and the sun was setting on Alexander's window of opportunity to sign it as well, her uncle had decided to let his guard down a little.

Or perhaps he'd given her a chance to prove once again that she wasn't on his side after all.

She'd spent time at the estate the week before, but she wasn't clear how to find her way through the sprawling mansion to her uncle's office, which she'd never wanted to find before. Unsure where to start her search for her uncle's desk, and unsure whether it was even a search worth embarking on, Lily prayed silently as she made her way down the richly carpeted hallway. *Dear God, if I shouldn't be doing this, please stop me. I don't know which way I should turn.*

She paused at a fork in the hallway, and the scripture she'd read two days before echoed through her mind. *Whether you turn to the right or to the left, your ears will hear a voice behind you, saying, "This is the way; walk in it."*

Attuning her ears to whatever words might come, Lily heard nothing.

She studied the two paths for some signal, any indication of which way she should go.

Muffled footsteps sounded behind her, and Lily spun around to see a plump woman in a maid's uniform pushing a cart up the hall.

"Trying to decide which way to go?" the crinkly eyed woman asked her.

"Yes. I'm afraid I still don't know my way around here very well."

"Where are you trying to get to?"

It was an innocent question, but Lily didn't have an innocent answer, and a blush crept up her cheeks while she tried frantically to think of a plausible answer. "I, um, just need to get out and get some air." It wasn't until she'd spoken that Lily remembered she'd just come in from outside.

The woman had dimpled elbows and dimpled cheeks and didn't stop working while she spoke. "Front door's the other way." She pulled a card from a hook on her cart, stuck it in the magnetic key-card reading slot of the door nearest her, and when the red light changed to green, she let herself into the suite before hanging the key on a tiny hook again.

Lily watched the woman disappear into the room, then looked at the inauspicious card.

Was it a master key that accessed all the rooms?

The maid carried a wastebasket from the room toward her cart.

Lily hurried down the hall. She couldn't take the woman's key card, not without being caught. And if her uncle even suspected she was up to something, he'd surely lock her up again.

Coming around a curve in the hallway, Lily finally recognized where she was. On one side of the hallway, wide windows overlooked the central fountain and curved driveway of the front courtyard. Beyond the high stone walls the city of Sardis shone like gold in the sinking evening sun. Come midnight, it would be too late for Alec to sign the covenant that would allow him to rule in the oligarchy with his sisters.

Isabelle and Anastasia would be outnumbered.

Lily blinked, and realized that among the soldiers who were stationed at regular intervals throughout the courtyard, her father and uncle were deep in conversation with men outside. Her uncle still hadn't let his little brother out of his sight.

But how long might they stay outside?

Turning to the opposite wall, Lily recognized the door to her uncle's office, and realized with a sinking heart that the solid double doors were latched with a magnetic-strip-reading card key lock. Of course her uncle wouldn't keep his private office open for anyone to wander in.

The sound of the maid's humming filled the hall.

"This is the way; walk in it."

Lily looked outside to where her uncle and father still stood, then darted down the hall toward the maid's cart, thinking quickly.

She couldn't steal the key card. There was no way—she'd only get caught and get in worse trouble. Besides, she couldn't imagine that God would want her to steal the key card.

"This is the way; walk in it."

Lily smiled as the woman pulled rolls of toilet paper from the shelf under her cart.

"Still trying to get somewhere?" The gray-haired woman smiled back.

"Yes, and I just realized—" Lily turned on her most hopeful, pleading look "—I don't have a key to get where I'm going. Could I borrow yours—" she pointed to the card "—if I promise to bring it right back?"

"I just work here." The woman chuckled. "Your uncle owns the place." She handed over the card. "I'm going to need that for the next room."

"How soon?"

"Takes me twenty minutes to do up a room right."

"I'll have it back to you in half that." Lily

promised as she held the card tight in her hand. "Thank you."

The woman resumed humming as Lily darted back down the hall. Would the key work on her uncle's office door? She could only pray that it would.

With another glance out the window, Lily saw that her father and uncle were no longer standing in the courtyard. Had they come inside?

Unable to answer that question, Lily figured it didn't matter anyway. She only had the card for ten minutes, and might not get a chance to borrow it again. Giving in to the mounting sense of urgency fueled by her pounding heart, she slipped the card into the slot.

A tiny green light lit on the handle, and she pulled it open quickly before it could go red, stepping inside her uncle's office and pulling the door shut quickly behind her.

The room smelled faintly of leather, the sweet cigars in the humidor and her uncle's cologne— a potent scent that smacked of her uncle's many betrayals. The instant it hit her nostrils she wanted to turn and run.

But she slipped the card into her pocket and headed for the desk. In the pure sunlight that filtered in through the generous windows, Lily had plenty of light to see. She hurried to her uncle's desk. There was no telling how soon her uncle might return, but she got the sense from the cologne-infused air that he spent much of his time in the room.

He could return at any moment.

Running her fingers along the center desk drawer, she felt a tiny latch give way at the gentle pressure of her thumb, and the bottom of the drawer swung loose, pivoting outward toward her, just deep enough to accommodate the thin sheaf of papers hidden inside.

Lily plucked them up. Were these the abdication documents? If she was able to get these to Alec or his sisters, would they be able to prove their family's right to the throne and end the political turmoil that kept Lydia in upheaval? Would her uncle finally be kept from power? She prayed it might be so.

Wanting to tuck the pages in some hidden spot to sneak them out, she realized she hadn't brought a bag or anything else to put them in.

But that realization quickly became irrelevant when she heard the rumble of men's voices just outside the door.

That was her uncle's cold laugh—she'd recognize it anywhere.

Glancing at the lock, she saw the light turn from red to green, and looked desperately around the room for somewhere to hide.

* * *

There was no furniture in the room, nothing but solid cement walls, cement floor, even a cement ceiling above his head. Alec paced the narrow space and watched through the tiny barred window as the sun sank lower in the sky, taking with it any chance he had to sign the covenant and support his family's claim to the crown. By midnight, his window of opportunity would close.

He couldn't blame Parliament for putting a time limit on signatures. The way he understood it, they were just trying to avoid any more squabbling. They had hundreds of years of Lydian laws and history to abide by—creating the ruling oligarchy had stretched those rules enough already. But they'd found a way to honor the law that allowed only descendants of Lydia on the throne, while at the same time avoiding the likelihood of crowning the wrong person before the rightful heir could be established.

They'd done the best they could do, given the circumstances, and placing a deadline on signatures was simply their way of promising the Lydian people that the uncertainty would end.

No, he was the one who'd failed everyone. Even his little sisters had gotten along better than he had. As he paced, his determination grew. Somehow, he'd find a way out of the Bardici estate.

Somehow, he'd make it to the Hall of Justice. But how could he possibly get there by midnight when he couldn't even find a way out of his room?

Lily spotted a small door beyond her uncle's desk and ducked into the space behind it, pulling the door shut after her just as she heard her father and uncle step into the office. Hardly daring to breathe, she prayed the men would leave quickly so she could get the papers to Alec or his sisters before sunset. Since she had no idea how she was going to smuggle them out of the Bardici estate, she knew she had to hurry.

But the voices of her father and uncle rumbled from the other side of the door.

"It doesn't matter. Lily certainly didn't know anything about it—the polygraph backed up her story. I couldn't beat a confession out of Alexander the last time I tried. Even if he knows where it is, he's made it clear he'd never going to tell anyone. It's quite simple. Alexander is a liability I can no longer afford. As long as he's alive, there's a chance he could retake the throne."

Lily stared at the richly stained wood door as the meaning behind her uncle's words sunk in.

They were going to kill Alec.

She couldn't let that happen. With trembling hands, she lowered the pages she held. Critical as they may have seemed a moment before, now they hardly mattered. Granted, she still felt the crown ought to be restored to Alec's family, but far, far more importantly, she had to do something to save Alec's life.

Still praying, she took a step back from the door, and bumped into something. She felt the oblong item with her hands. It was smooth, a little higher than counter height, with buttons on a panel toward the front. She realized the closet she'd stepped into was an office workroom.

A plan formed in her mind.

A foolish, crazy plan.

Her uncle held no esteem for her life. As long as he didn't care whether she lived or died, she had nothing to bargain with.

But he cared about the papers she held. He'd do anything to keep them from falling into the wrong hands.

She waited until her uncle's fading voice told her he'd left his office again, then quickly got to work. He'd said little to indicate when he planned to murder Alec, but Lily got the distinct impression it would be soon.

She didn't have much time.

Alec heard footsteps approaching.

Good enough. The sun had already begun to

set, but from what Titus and Julian had told him, he had until midnight to reach the Hall of Justice. He braced himself near the door, ready for whatever came his way. At this point, he was desperate enough to take whatever break he could get, no matter what risks might be involved.

He only had until midnight.

The door opened, and the dying light illuminated the faces of Titus and Julian.

Alec relaxed slightly. They were his only known allies. He wasn't going to attack them.

"Bring him this way." David Bardici's voice echoed from the hallway. "We're going to have one last negotiation session."

The soldiers cuffed him on either side, shackling their wrists to his, and followed Bardici up to the back courtyard. Flaming torches illuminated smooth walls towering twenty feet around, topped with parapets and gun-wielding soldiers.

In fact, as Alec's eyes adjusted and he looked around, he saw that men with guns rimmed the ground and the wall, a double layer of muzzles pointed directly at him.

Bardici wasn't taking any chances.

The general pulled out a handgun and stood opposite him no more than two meters away. In a low voice, too quiet for the men who rimmed the courtyard to hear, he began. "I'll make this simple. I will ask you a question. If you do not answer to my satisfaction, I'll shoot you—not a deadly shot, but something that will hurt enough to jog your memory.

"If I have to ask my question again, and if you don't answer to my satisfaction, I'll shoot you again. We'll keep going like that until I have the information I need, or you die, whichever happens first. Got that?"

"Yes," Alec answered with a sinking heart. He had a good feeling he knew exactly what the question was going to be. And he knew he wouldn't have an answer that would satisfy the madman who faced him.

Lily returned the key to the maid with extra thanks and headed down the hallway almost at a run. The sprawling mansion was quiet. Too quiet.

She had to find her uncle.

Bounding down the wide front stairs with the sheaf of papers in her right hand, she came around the corner and almost slammed into her mother.

"Lily!" Sandra Bardici looked more upset than startled. "What do you think you're doing?"

"I need to find Uncle David. It's important."

"What?" Her mother took hold of her right wrist and turned the pages so she could read them. The color drained from her face. "Where did you get these?"

"It doesn't matter. I need—"

"No. You don't." Her mother's grip on her wrist tightened, and she pulled her back toward the stairs. "You're coming with me."

Lily tried to pry her arm away, but her mother's grip was surprisingly strong, and her attitude uncharacteristically fierce. What had happened to the obsequious woman Lily had known all her life? "Mom, you don't understand."

"No, *you* don't understand. Your uncle David is within hours of taking the power he was born to control. You're not going to do anything to stop him." She pulled her toward the stairway. "He's going to be king."

"But Uncle David can't be allowed to become king."

"Don't say that!" Her mother slapped her across the cheek. "I've put up with your insolence long enough. Your uncle David will be king, and I will be his queen. And no one—not you, not your pathetic excuse for a father, nobody will take that away from me!"

Lily blinked back the tears that had sprung to her eyes at her mother's sudden swipe. It took her a moment to make sense of what Sandra Bardici was saying, but slowly, the pieces fell into place. "You're on Uncle David's side?"

"I have been for years, Lily. Who do you think had the foresight to invest in the Bardici bid for the throne? Certainly not your father. No, I've done it all myself, even when I had to go behind his back. I sold everything, and when he refused to sell, I did what needed to be done to liquidate our assets." She pulled Lily up the steps after her.

Shocked by her mother's words, Lily didn't resist her pull up the stairs. "You poisoned the horses because Dad wouldn't sell them?"

"*Somebody* had to do it. We couldn't afford to keep them alive."

"You killed my horses." Anger snapped inside her, and Lily jerked her hand free, pivoting back down the stairs. She had to find her uncle David. She had to stop him, before he became king and her mother, queen.

"Lily, no!" Her mother lunged after her, but she was still several steps higher on the stairway, and Lily bounded down the last five stairs in a single leap.

Her mother grabbed at the empty air, but her momentum was too great for her, and she keeled over the edge of the railing, falling the last ten feet onto the marble floor below. "No!" she screamed. "You'll pay for this!"

Judging by the racket her mother was making, Lily figured the woman hadn't been injured too badly. She ran down the back hall searching for her father, her uncle or anyone who could tell her where the men had gone.

* * *

David Bardici pointed the gun at Alec. "Where is the Scepter of Charlemagne?"

Alec debated how best to answer. Was there any point trying to lead the man on in a satisfactory way? "If I give you an answer, how will you know I'm telling the truth?"

"You will tell me the truth, or you will die!" Bardici took aim with his gun, and before Alec even realized the man wasn't bluffing, he sent a shot into Alec's left shoe.

Pain speared up through his foot, and he sagged slightly, but quickly straightened.

The general stared at him with rage-reddened eyes and nearly screamed his question as he asked again. "Where is the Scepter of Charlemagne?"

Alec looked down at the blood that had begun to seep from his injured foot into the pale pink cobblestones of the courtyard. How many more shots could he take?

It didn't matter.

He had no choice. He lifted his head and faced Bardici. "I will never tell you."

Bardici took aim at Alec's other foot just as a female voice carried through the courtyard.

"Wait!"

Lily followed the sound of the gunshot and nearly flung herself into the midst of the armed men. "Don't shoot." She waved the papers as she skidded to a stop in front of Alec, facing her uncle. "This man is under my protection."

David Bardici sneered. "I can shoot you as easily as him."

"You wouldn't dare." Lily lifted Basil's abdication documents high in her hand. "These papers prove that Basil renounced any claim to the throne. Alec and his family are the rightful rulers of Lydia." She blinked upward, surprised by how many armed soldiers surrounded them, then smiled. "And now every Lydian soldier here knows that Prince Alexander is the rightful heir, not you."

"Give me those!" David lunged for the papers.

Lily flung her arm backward to keep the documents from his grasp. The two soldiers handcuffed to either side of Alec lifted him back and away. Lily tried to follow them, but their retreat was too slow for her uncle. He snatched the papers from her hand as he whipped his gun toward her.

At that moment, her father stepped in between them, pushing his big brother backward, away from Lily. "Don't touch her!" he yelled, shoving the general away.

David raised his gun and Michael grabbed his wrist, grappling with him, the gun pointed high in the air, neither man in control.

As David struggled with his brother, the general called out to the soldiers standing by. "Shoot him! Shoot Alexander!"

Lily turned to face Alec as the soldiers who were handcuffed to his wrists unlocked the cuffs, though they still held him up as he sagged between them. She had no way of knowing how much blood he'd lost, but judging by the pool of red that stained the cobblestones, he could bleed out in short order. She needed to help him.

"Shoot him, I said!" David screamed, still struggling with his brother for control of the gun.

"Alec?" a soldier called down from the wall, "should we shoot General Bardici?"

Alec looked up with a weak smile toward the voice that had spoken. "He needs to stand trial for his crimes. Capture him." In spite of the strain in his voice that betrayed the seriousness of his injury, his words carried clearly, and the men on the ground rushed forward.

"Not so fast!" Sandra Bardici limped forward from the doorway, her gun trained on Alec. "If anybody moves, I'll blow him away."

The sight of his wife wielding a gun must have startled Michael, because he faltered, and David quickly got the upper hand—control of the gun and the papers he'd snatched away from Lily.

David backed toward his sister-in-law.

"Sandra?" Michael looked at her in dismay as she pointed the gun toward their group.

A sneer traced across his wife's face. "It's over, Michael. I've waited long enough. I'm leaving you for your brother." David shuffled sideways until he stood beside her, then lifted the papers he'd taken from Lily to where a flaming torch burned brightly, fire illuminating the courtyard.

The papers burst into flame, the orange tongues licking upward toward David's hand until he dropped the black wisps of ashes to the ground.

With triumphant smiles, David and Sandra darted into the house.

Lily dropped down at Alec's feet. Whatever else was going on, Alec had to have his injury attended to. There wasn't time to worry about the documents, her mother's sudden revelation or anything else.

A few soldiers moved forward uncertainly.

"I need a first-aid kit," Lily told them as she worked Alec's shoe from his foot as quickly and gently as she could. "And he needs something to drink—juice or soda, something to replace the fluids and blood sugar he's losing."

The soldiers scrambled away, and the two who stood on either side of Alec lowered him to the ground.

"I need to get to the Hall of Justice." Alec looked as though he'd crawl away if only he could gather his strength.

"You're not going anywhere until this injury

is taken care of, or you'll pass out before you get there." Lily peeled back his bloody sock to reveal a clean shot through the foot. Fortunately it was straightforward—the bullet had passed straight through—but it had sliced several vessels that were losing blood quickly.

Soldiers appeared with first-aid kits, and Lily quickly located a tourniquet, wrapping it above the wound. "You're going to need to have those veins repaired, Alec. We'll have to get you to the hospital." She looked him full in the face.

A soldier held a bottle of juice for him, and Alec swallowed a few gulps. "I need to get to the Hall of Justice by midnight. How much time do we have?"

The man at his right arm checked his watch. "Twenty minutes. If we hurry, we might just make it."

Realizing the importance of the trip and Alec's determination to do his part to help his family, Lily quickly bandaged the wound, tying it off with as much pressure as she could to staunch any further loss of blood. "This should hold you for now, but I want you admitted to the hospital as soon as you get that paper signed, do you understand?"

Appreciation shimmered in Alec's eyes. "Thank you. I have to get going."

As she tied off the bandage, Lily told him all she knew. "My uncle and the other Lydian generals are working for someone who goes by the number 8. You're going to have to stop them all before this will end." She stood, and the soldiers eased Alec to standing.

"Take it easy," she told him. "I'm going to get the documents."

"Your uncle already burned them up."

"Those were only copies." She cast a quick smile over her shoulder as she ran toward the house.

Lily left Alec in the care of the soldiers. She didn't want to leave his side, but at the same time, she needed to produce the real abdication documents to prove her uncle had no right to rule. Besides, she didn't feel she had any right to be close to him after the way her uncle had used her to get to Alec. The only way she knew to make up for her role in his capture was to do what she could to help his family.

That meant retrieving the papers she'd hidden inside.

As Lily hurried through the dark halls, she heard footsteps behind her and glanced over her shoulder, but didn't see anyone. Was she being followed?

Ducking back into a doorway, she watched as a figure ran past in the darkness, only recognizing her father after he had passed.

Where was he headed? Unwilling to be deterred from reclaiming the critical documents, Lily took the next corner to the spot where she'd tucked the papers under a hallway rug. She skidded to a stop just as a voice sounded behind her.

"Lillian. How nice of you to join us."

Spinning around, she watched her uncle pass through the filtered moonlight that poured in through a window, the gun in his hand glinting silver in the darkness. Lily froze. She didn't dare reach for the papers now or she'd give away their location.

"I was hoping we wouldn't have to leave you behind. You're far, far too handy to have around." David advanced, holding the gun on her, and grabbed her by the wrist.

"Are you coming?" Sandra rounded the corner, spotted them both, and smiled wickedly. "Ah, perfect. Let's bring her with. The copter's ready. Come on."

With her uncle dragging her by the arm and her mother prodding her in the back with the gun, Lily had no choice but to go with them. They turned down the hallway where her father had disappeared moments before. She almost missed him standing in the shadows of a darkened doorway, but she caught his eye as she struggled past.

"Help! Help me!"

"Shut up. No one can hear you anyway." Her mother rammed the gun into her back.

As they made the next corner, Lily looked back in time to see her father dart silently from the doorway in the other direction.

He was running away.

FOURTEEN

Alec rested most of his weight on Titus and Julian as he hopped quickly toward the car. They didn't have a moment to lose. Even with the streets empty in the middle of the night, it would likely take them all of fifteen minutes to reach the Hall of Justice.

And then he still had to get inside.

A soldier ran ahead, opening the car door for him, and Alec balanced himself on the open door as he ducked in.

"Alec!" Panic infused the familiar voice behind him, and Alec turned to see Lily's father Michael running toward them. "They have Lily! They're taking her with them!"

"Who?" Alec's stomach plunged.

Michael's answer didn't surprise him. "Sandra and David. They're holding guns on her—they mentioned a helicopter."

Titus grimaced. "The copter's in the front courtyard. Get in the car. It's fastest this way."

Alec dived into the backseat. "To the front court-yard!" he screamed at the driver.

The man put the car in gear and peeled out. "I thought we were going to the Hall of Justice."

Alec's heart clenched. If he went after Lily, there might not be time to make it to the Hall of Justice by midnight. But if her armed uncle took her, he might never see her again.

Not alive, anyway.

There would have to be time for both. "The front courtyard," he repeated. "Quickly!"

Tires squealed as the driver took the corner at a tight clip. Titus and Julian hadn't taken the time to get in, but ran behind the car as they cleared the corner of the mansion.

Alec had the door open as the car squealed to a stop. He leapt out on his good foot, balancing his weight on the open door. Ahead of him the cop-ter's rotors surged through the night air as Sandra shoved Lily ahead of her through the open side door of the helicopter.

"Alec!" Lily screamed at him, but arms reached through the door and jerked her in.

Sandra spun around with her gun, shooting wildly in his direction before diving inside the aircraft just as it lifted off.

Boots skidded across the cobblestones as Alec's fellow soldiers came to a stop.

Already the helicopter was high above them. There was no way to reach them.

Lily was gone.

He'd failed her.

Alec pounded a fist impatiently on the hood of the car, then turned to his friends. "Get in. We've got to hurry if we're going to make it to the Hall of Justice."

Titus and Julian piled into the car with him, and the driver took off. Alec watched the digital minutes on the dashboard clock moving relentlessly closer to midnight.

11:53 p.m.

11:54 p.m.

They entered the city with three minutes to go before midnight, and Alec felt sick fear creep up from his stomach. Though the men had been silent so far, Julian offered, "Perhaps they won't mind if you're a few minutes late."

11:58 p.m.

11:59 p.m.

They squealed to a stop in front of the Hall of Justice at 12:02 a.m., and Titus jumped out, pulling on the double doors, which didn't budge.

"Try the side doors," he suggested, piling back in.

They pulled around the corner in time to see the red taillights of another car pulling away.

Titus jumped out again and checked the doors

while Julian leapt out the other side and waved at the car that had just pulled away ahead of them.

The taillights blinked as the car shifted into reverse, coming to a stop just in front of them. A man stepped out, and Alec recognized Kirk Covington, the man who'd been accused of killing his brother Thaddeus six years before.

Alec hauled himself out of the backseat. "Kirk!" He tried to call out, but was disappointed by the weakness in his voice and the stars that danced across his vision at the sudden exertion of standing.

"Alec?" Kirk trotted toward him. "Is that you?"

"Am I too late?"

Kirk shook his head regretfully. "We had to beg them to keep the building open until the clock chimed midnight. There was nothing we could do after that."

"Alec?" A female voice pierced the night, and Alec watched his little sister Anastasia emerge from the car ahead of his. She ran toward him and threw herself into his arms.

Alec slumped against the car, nearly toppled by the petite princess.

"Careful!" Julian warned her.

Concern filled Stasi's face. "Are you okay? You look awful." She patted his cheek.

"I barely made it here." Alec felt himself waver, and he looked at the locked doors. "I didn't make it here in time."

The realization sunk in slowly as he watched the excitement on his sister's face turn to disappointment.

He had arrived too late. He'd failed his family. He'd failed everyone.

Leaning heavily on the doorframe, he fought to keep his eyes open.

"Alec?" Stasi's voice seemed to come from far away. "Are you okay?"

And from even farther away, he heard Julian say, "We need to get him to the hospital."

"We should be glad the Bardicis have fled," Levi Grenaldo insisted as he paced in the small hospital room. "The three of them have a majority over Isabelle and Stasi, but as long as they're afraid to show their faces, they won't be able to exercise their right to rule."

Alec groaned impatiently from his hospital bed. Thankful as he was that his sisters and their new fiancés had filled him in on all that had happened, he still didn't like what he was hearing. "Parliament won't budge on the forty-eight-hour rule?"

"I felt foolish asking." Isabelle wrapped her arms around Levi and stilled his pacing. "They've done all they can to support us, but they've got the United Nations looking over their shoulder and the media criticizing their every move. They can't change a rule two days after they made it.

They'd lose all their authority in the eyes of the people and the nations of the world."

"Then we've got to find Lillian." Alec swung his legs around to the side of his bed.

"Oh, no." Kirk lifted his feet by the ankles and spun him back around again. "We've been over this already. Just be glad she's gone."

Alec sat up higher and stared Kirk down. In spite of Stasi's reassurances that their brother, Thaddeus, was still alive, Alec still wasn't completely over the six-year grudge he'd held against the man who'd been accused of killing Lydia's heir. He glared at the man who'd proposed to his sister the day before. "What would you do if they had Stasi locked away somewhere?" He turned to Levi. "How would you feel if Isabelle had been taken?"

He looked back and forth between them. "Lily risked her life for me."

Isabelle shook her head. "She's a Bardici. She's the enemy."

"She is *not* the enemy," Alec seethed. How could he make them understand? "As long as David Bardici remains at large our family will never reclaim the throne."

Everyone was silent for a moment before Stasi sighed. "We don't even know where they've taken her."

Hope fluttered its weak wings inside his heart. "We haven't been able to find her anywhere in

Lydia. That leaves only one likely place—Bardici's compound in the North African desert."

"But we have no authority there, no allies on the ground." Levi was a lawyer specializing in international law and Isabelle's new fiancé. He stepped closer to Alec's bedside. "From what you've told us, Bardici's compound is manned by Lydian soldiers. If they're under his control, you can be sure he won't have told them anything that would make them question his orders. He has every advantage over us."

"Levi's right," Kirk concurred. "Even if Bardici only has a few dozen men at his disposal, we'd need a team at least as big to secure his stronghold. How are we going to transport that many men there? We're down to one helicopter."

"Sanctuary International has helicopters," Isabelle began, referring to the organization Levi's family operated, which had helped her escape the ambush.

Her fiancé cut her off. "Not in the vicinity. By the time we arrange to have them flown here, we might as well fly commercially into Tripoli and rent a bus to the compound."

"Aah." Alec made an impatient noise and swung his legs over the side of the bed again. "I'm not going to sit here bickering while Lillian is imprisoned by her uncle. I've let you all down by not signing the document. The only way I can make things right is by bringing Bardici into custody with Lillian's testimony to put him away for his crimes."

His sisters and their fiancés exchanged worried looks.

"But Alec?" Stasi questioned softly. "How can you be so sure she'll testify against him?"

Alec rose shakily onto his one good foot. "I will find her. And then you won't have to question her allegiance anymore."

Lily knotted the bedsheets to the curtains and let them fall past the balcony almost to the ground. If Alec had made it climbing up, she could make it climbing down. And then she'd find him. She'd get back to Lydia somehow, and give Alec the papers that proved her uncle had no right to rule. And maybe, if she was really lucky, he'd be willing to overlook all the nasty lies her uncle had told about her intentionally betraying him.

The sheets held as she climbed down, and she hurried through the night across the open sand, mindful of the dangers of the desert that Alec had taught her about. She had a single bottle of water, and knew where to find the trickling waterfall where they'd left the horses. Would the animals still be there, or would they have given up and gone in search of more plentiful forage? For their own sakes, she prayed they'd be okay.

* * *

The rotor blades sliced the evening air as Alec leaned his head through the open door of the helicopter, his binoculars trained on Bardici's compound looming on the horizon. His eyes landed on a familiar sight—the knotted sage green window curtains extending from a window.

"That's Lily's signal. She's there."

"She has a signal?" Titus questioned him. He and Julian had agreed to accompany him along with four other men—the maximum number their copter could safely carry.

"Is she expecting us?" Julian asked. "It might be another trap."

Alec leaned against the doorframe as the helicopter moved toward the compound. "I'm not going to ask any of you to go in—" he began.

"We *volunteered* for this mission," Julian reminded him. "We just want to know what we're getting into."

"There's no way of knowing until we're on the ground," Titus reminded his friend. "When Kirk and Levi tried to come along, we told them they needed to stay behind to keep the princesses safe. We told them we'd take care of it. So, let's take care of it."

Alec grinned at the soldiers. "You two are better friends than I deserve."

"Nah." Titus shoved him in the shoulder. "We

just don't want you to do anything stupid, like trying to head in alone. You don't need another injury."

"Take it easy on that foot," Julian insisted, nodding at the stiff walking boot that allowed Alec to hobble, however gracelessly, without further injuring his foot.

The helicopter sank toward the ground inside the compound courtyard. Alec and his men had gone over their plan and its contingencies plenty of times.

They were Lydian soldiers. Bardici's men were Lydian soldiers, too. Alec had an order, signed by his sisters and Michael Bardici—the ruling representatives of the monarchy according to the Oligarchy Covenant outlined by Parliament—removing David Bardici from his post as the General of Lydia's army. He also had a warrant to arrest the man for treason.

Whether the men at the distant outpost were aware of the events that had unfolded in Lydia, and whether they would recognize the order remained to be seen. If the soldiers opted to follow their general, Alec and his men would be easily overcome by the forces that outnumbered them.

Armed soldiers surrounded the copter before the skids touched down.

As planned, Julian and Titus exited first. As high-ranking officers who had recently been stationed at the compound, their authority was quickly recognized, and they explained to the men on the ground the need to capture Bardici.

To Alec's immense relief, the soldiers grinned at the news, and saluted him when he stepped from the copter.

"This way." One of the men on the ground waved them toward the building. "We'll have to move quickly."

Alec hobbled after the men as they poured into the building. He heard shouting up ahead, and wished he could move fast enough to see what was happening. When he came around the corner of the hallway, he found the men clustered around a closed door.

"Bardici's in there." Julian waved him forward. "He ran in just ahead of us with a woman beside him. They've barricaded themselves inside."

"David Bardici," Alec called. "You have been removed from your post and are wanted on charges of treason. Come out nicely, or we'll shoot the door down."

"You don't dare shoot into this room," David Bardici's unmistakable voice called back. "I have Lillian in here with me. If you ever want to see her alive again, you'll go back to where you came from."

The Arabian filly pranced nervously under Lillian as she tried to hold her still, inching closer to her uncle's compound in hopes of catching a glimpse of the helicopter that had landed.

Was it Lydian? She thought she recognized the helicopter, but she wasn't nearly an expert on flying machines. Still, she wasn't about to leave the area if there was any chance that Alec or his men were aboard the craft. Without a passport or any money, she didn't know how she was ever going to get back to Sardis. The helicopter could be a godsend. She prayed God would give her wisdom, even as the half-wild horse beneath her trotted unbidden toward the fortress that loomed above the desert.

"Lillian?" Alec called from where he crouched with his men on either side of the doorway, protected by the sturdy stone walls from anything those inside might shoot at them. "If you're in there, tell me you're okay."

Silence.

David laughed. "She's in no position to speak right now."

Alec's stomach sank. What did the tyrant's cryptic response mean? Had he already disposed of Lily? Alec couldn't bear the thought. And yet, how else could he explain her lack of response?

He looked at his men. "Did you see Lillian go in there with him?"

"We came around the corner right behind him.

He had a female with him, but I didn't get a close look." The soldier answered in a hushed whisper.

"Can anyone ID the woman who was with him?"

With regret on their faces, the soldiers shook their heads.

Alec pinched his eyes shut. Had Lily gone willingly with her uncle? "Was the female showing any sign of resistance?"

The soldier nearest him answered without hesitation. "She appeared to be accompanying him of her own free will."

FIFTEEN

Three soldiers rode out on horseback toward her. Lily wanted to rein her horse in, but the wild filly refused to be controlled. Besides, the armed men had clearly already spotted her, so there would be little point in trying to run away.

"Halt." The lead rider raised his gun.

At the sight of the automatic rifle, the filly had the good sense to come to a stop.

"Lily?" one of the soldiers asked.

"Yes."

"How did you get out here?"

Before she could explain, another soldier pulled close to her horse, grabbing the halter. "You need to come with us."

Silently, so that Bardici wouldn't hear, Alec dispensed the men in teams. "I want the windows to this room guarded. Don't let him escape. Make a sweep of the compound. I'm not convinced Lily is in that room."

Moments after he sent the last group of men down the hallway, Titus approached from the other direction, motioning to Alec with his finger. "This way."

Though reluctant to leave the room where Bardici was barricaded, Alec hobbled around the corner in time to see three men leading a smaller, feminine figure.

"Shh." The soldiers shushed them both as Lily stifled her squeal upon seeing him.

David Bardici's shout echoed down the hallway. "If you want to see Lillian alive again, you and your men will back away from this door."

Alec pulled Lily into his arms as he turned back to respond to the man's threats. "I repeat, David Bardici, you have been removed from your post and are wanted on charges of treason."

"You don't have the authority to arrest me! The monarchy is head of the armed forces, and the Bardicis have a ruling majority on the oligarchy council."

"Do they?" Alec questioned loudly as his men began to gather again in the hallway. With Lily safe in his arms, he had no qualms blasting his way past the general's barricade, though he'd prefer to take him without a fight. He didn't want to risk the lives of the men who trusted him to lead them.

"Of course we do!" David shouted from the

other side of the door. "The Bardicis have three against two."

"No, Uncle David," Lily called out from under the protective drape of Alec's arm. "At best, you have two against three. I will always side with the Royal House of Lydia."

Knowing Lily's words had exposed David's sole negotiating point as a desperate bluff, Alec lifted his gun, motioning to his men to draw their weapons and stand behind where he stood, closest to the doors. "This is your final warning. Come out—"

But before he could finish his sentence, the doors burst open, revealing David standing in the doorway, holding Sandra Bardici in front of him, his gun pressed to her neck.

"Stand down," Bardici shouted at the soldiers, his eyes roving crazily until they landed on Lily, tucked almost out of sight in Alec's shadow less than a meter from where he stood. The sneer of a smile bent his lips. "Lillian, you will tell these soldiers to fall back, or you will never see your mother alive again."

Lily tensed against him, and Alec could feel her warring with how to respond.

It was a call he couldn't ask her to make.

Moving quickly, deftly, he executed the move he'd replayed in his mind since the moment the general had pulled a gun on Lily on her father's boat. His hand snapped forward, jerking the gun away from the general.

Just as quickly, Sandra Bardici lunged toward the weapon.

"Mother, no!" Lily screamed, darting out from under Alec's arm to stop her mother.

Alec couldn't let her step past the shield of his body armor. He turned his back on the Bardicis, covering Lily as a gun went off behind him.

When he spun around again a second later, David Bardici had crumpled to the floor, and the soldiers on the other side of the doorway leaped forward to restrain Sandra, pulling the gun easily from her trembling hands.

"Mother?" Lily gasped, looking down at her prone, bloodied uncle on the floor, and then back up to her mother.

But Sandra sneered down at David. "You'll never pull a gun on me again!"

The soldiers led her away, while Titus crouched by the general's side and checked his pulse. "He's gone."

"And with him, any answers he might have given us about the elusive 8." Alec looked in the direction the men had taken Sandra. "I wonder if that's why she felt she had to kill him?"

"She won't tell you anything," Lily predicted. "But my father—"

"Your father has been cooperative ever since your mother left him."

"I don't know how much he knows, though. In many ways, I think he was his brother's puppet, not a knowledgeable conspirator."

Alec pulled her close against him, taking comfort in the knowledge that he'd kept her safe. That she'd taken a stand on his side.

But would his siblings agree?

"Let's get things closed up here and get back to Lydia."

Lily focused on breathing slowly, evenly, as she accompanied Alec onboard her uncle's helicopter. After refueling the copter he and his men had arrived in, Alec had sent Sandra back to Lydia in the custody of his men. Grateful for the use of the second Lydian helicopter, Lily felt relieved that she didn't have to face her mother for the ride home.

She tried to tell herself everything would be fine, even though her mother had left her father and shot her uncle. Even though she was still deep in debt and could easily be charged with treason for signing the oligarchy covenant at her uncle's orders.

"How's your foot?" she asked Alec as he situated himself in the seat and the copter lifted off.

He didn't answer, but settled his gaze on her face. She felt a blush rise to her cheeks, and tried to shake it off. "I'm so sorry. I'm sorry my uncle shot you, that my family has been attacking yours—"

His hand slid over hers. "I'm sorry, too."

"What's going to happen?"

"I don't know. It's all up in the air, isn't it? My father's still in a coma, my brother, Thaddeus, is still missing. As near as I can tell, the only way to ultimately resolve the question of the crown is to find my brother. He's the only one who knows where to find the Scepter of Charlemagne."

"The Scepter of Charlemagne." Lily immediately recalled her uncle asking her about it. "Why is it so important?"

"The crowned head of Lydia has always held the scepter. There's a document inside the scepter that has been signed by every monarch in the history of the kingdom. Whoever holds the scepter controls the crown."

Lily let out a slow breath. "No wonder my uncle was so determined to get his hands on it. But how are we ever going to find it? No one even knows where Thaddeus is."

"Kirk thinks he may be able to locate him, but it could take a while."

"What's going to happen until then?"

Alec offered her a cautious smile. "The ruling oligarchy will remain in place until Thaddeus is crowned. With your uncle dead, that leaves you and your dad to rule along with my sisters."

"But won't we be charged with treason for conspiring with my uncle?"

"To my knowledge, you never conspired with David Bardici." Alec looked at her with trust in his eyes.

Lily felt her own eyes well with appreciative tears. "I never did—but Uncle David said all those terrible things—"

"Your uncle David was a terrible man. I don't believe any of the accusations he made against you. In the case of your father, however, it gets a little trickier." Alec conceded, "But, if he can give us information that would lead us to this 8, if he can help us end this once and for all, I'm sure he could get a lighter sentence. Now your mother, on the other hand—"

Lily shuddered. "She murdered my uncle."

"It could be classified as self-defense."

"She murdered my horses. All this time, I thought she was a sycophant, going along with whatever my father or uncle said. But she was playing them just to get her own way." Lily thought for a little while longer, realizing that her uncle had tried to paint *her* as just such a character. Alec said he didn't believe the terrible things her uncle had said about her, but in light of her mother's actions, Lily still felt the burden of proof. "My uncle accused me of behaving that way."

"He said you deliberately made me fall in love

with you so you could manipulate me and learn my secrets."

"I didn't—"

But Alec raised a finger to her mouth, shushing her. "If that's what you were trying to do, you were awful at it."

Her eyes widened. Was he saying he hadn't fallen in love with her after all?

"You didn't learn anything from me," Alec clarified. "You didn't ask me about any of the things your uncle wanted to know." He leaned closer to her over the armrest that separated their seats. "But, as far as falling in love with you…" He removed his finger from her lips and leaned closer.

Lily's mouth fell open. "I don't know if it's wise to act on feelings right now," she cautioned him. "You've got a country to reassure and a Parliament to placate. If they see you with me, how will they ever trust you?"

"I'm not part of the ruling oligarchy. You are. Perhaps they need to see you with me to know they can trust you."

"Be careful, Alec. Be very, very careful." She settled back into her seat.

Alec leaned back in his seat as well. "I will."

The sun was rising on a new day as the helicopter neared Sardis.

Lily realized what she needed to do. "Is there any way I can get to my uncle's estate?" she asked.

"Right now?"

"It's rather urgent."

Exhausted though he was, Alec didn't want Lily visiting the place alone. "We can land in the court-yard." He passed the order along to the pilot, then asked Lily, "What's so important that we've got to go now?"

"If we can prove that Basil abdicated, that will erase any question of whether your family has the right to rule Lydia, correct? This oligarchy non-sense can be done away with, and your family can be returned to the throne."

"But your uncle burned the abdication docu-ments." Alec had gotten enough of a glimpse of the papers as Lily and her uncle had waved them around to know they were the real thing.

"Trust me." Lily smiled as they arrived at the sprawling mansion.

Alec hesitated at the thought of trekking through the halls on his injured foot.

Lily must have realized how exhausted he was. "You can wait here. I'll be right back."

She hurried inside.

Alec stepped out and leaned against the copter, easing the pressure on his foot, and heard a vehicle approaching. Immediately on his guard, he was relieved to see his sisters and their fiancés jump out of the vehicle when it came to a stop.

"*There* you are," Isabelle accused him. "We've

all been going crazy waiting for you to return, and no sooner does your helicopter come into view than you head here."

"What are you doing here?" Stasi asked.

"Lily needed to get something."

"Couldn't it wait?"

He shrugged.

Kirk leaned against the car beside him and spoke in a conspiratorial tone. "On the night of the state dinner, you were supposed to learn about your next promotion, weren't you?"

"That's right. With everything else that's been going on, I almost forgot. But my promotion was arranged between my father, as head of the military, and General Bardici, the head of the army. Neither of them can tell us what they decided."

"Your sisters have been discussing it."

Isabelle smiled up at her brother. "We want you to be the new general in charge of the army."

Alec reeled back. "From lieutenant to general? That's quite a promotion."

"We don't know who else we can trust," Stasi explained. "Bardici's highest-ranking officers followed his orders—including orders against our family."

"We may never know for certain the extent of their allegiances." As Isabelle finished her statement, Lily burst from the building, papers in hand.

Alec watched his sisters eye her warily. He

knew they didn't trust her because she was a Bardici. "What have you got, Lily?"

She laid out the papers on the back of his sister's car. "These are Basil's original abdication documents. They prove that the members of your family have every right to the crown. The papers my uncle burned were only copies I made on aged paper. If he'd stopped to examine them under better light, he'd have realized he didn't have the originals." She looked at Alec with hope in her eyes. "These should restore your family to the throne."

"Are you sure?" Levi, the law expert, bent over the papers, studying them closely.

While he analyzed the documents, Stasi and Isabelle eyed each other over his head.

Isabelle raised an eyebrow.

Stasi turned to Lily. "Why would you help our family?"

Lily looked up at Alec, and he watched a familiar blush rise to her cheeks. "Your brother," she began softly, then bit her lip, unsure how much more to say.

Alec decided there was no longer any need to hide his feelings. If he was ever going to convince his family that Lily's devotion was true, this was his chance. "I'm in love with you, Lily Bardici."

Her face bunched up as though she wasn't sure whether she wanted to smile or cry. "After you watched my mother turn against my father and then my uncle?"

"You're not your mother." He took a step closer to her. "Nor are you your father or your uncle. You've suffered enough because of them. You don't have to pay for their crimes any longer."

Kirk cleared his throat and, to Alec's surprise, instead of questioning him, said, "I know what it's like to be falsely accused. And I know how much it means when those you care about believe in you."

Stasi beamed up at her fiancé as he wrapped an arm around her.

"If these documents prove that Basil abdicated…" Isabelle began.

"Then all we still lack is…" Stasi's words hung in the air.

"The Scepter of Charlemagne," Alec finished for his sister.

"Only one man knows where that is." Kirk pulled Stasi close.

No one spoke the name of Thaddeus aloud. No one had to.

"These papers are legitimate." Levi broke their silence. "They should stand up in any court. More than that, if I'm reading this passage correctly, it seems Basil didn't simply abdicate because he didn't want to rule. He left on his own terms in an agreement to keep his true parentage from being revealed."

"What does that mean?" Lily asked.

"It seems—" Levi looked at the papers again "—Basil wasn't the king's biological son. The king's first wife was unfaithful. Basil wasn't a true descendent of Lydia."

Lily squealed happily, and Alec gave her a questioning look.

"We're not related," she declared joyously.

"What?"

Her cheeks blushed red as Lily explained, "If Basil and your great-grandfather were half brothers, that meant you and I would be cousins of some sort."

"*Distant* cousins," Alec noted. He'd thought of that, but hadn't seen it as an issue. Apparently Lily had found it troubling. He was relieved that she no longer had to be concerned about it. "So, you're glad to learn that you don't really have any claim to the throne of Lydia?"

"I don't want the throne. I just want—" Lily looked at him with affection in her eyes, but her words dropped off as she glanced at his extended family gathered around them.

Isabelle smiled. "I don't think any of us are in any position to question Lily's allegiance any longer."

"In that case—" Alec grinned "—I need to rest my injured foot."

He dropped down on one knee, his injured foot stretched out behind him as he cupped Lily's hands in his. "Lily Bardici, would you marry me?"

Silent tears leaked down Lily's cheeks. "Are you sure, Alec?"

"More sure than I've ever been about anything. You helped me realize who I am. I want you by my side, always."

"Yes." Her voice was little more than a broken whisper, but it was enough for Alec. He stood again and kissed her while his sisters clapped.

"Welcome to the club," Kirk said with a playful shove.

"Welcome to the family," Isabelle and Stasi joined in.

"A real family," Lily whispered between kisses.

"A family that loves you," Alec promised. "No matter what happens."

He thought for a moment about the uncertainties that hung like a cloudy sky over their future. But like a beam of sunshine, his love for Lily was enough to light the way.

* * * * *

ACKNOWLEDGMENTS

Loads of people contributed their expertise to make this book possible, and I'm grateful to every one of them. Thanks especially to the Drs. Kent and Jodi Pulfer, who in addition to being lovely people and wonderful servants of God, can also list deadly horse diseases from off the tops of their heads. I am grateful to leech off your brilliance!

I'm indebted to the tremendously talented Marion Laird, who set the Lydian National Anthem to music—in Lydian mode, no less! Your contribution makes Lydia feel even more real.

As always, thank you to my phenomenal husband, Ray, who patiently listens as I try to sort out character motivation, reads my manuscripts and gently reminds me that, fond as I may be of writing them, sentences of more than a few dozen words aren't appealing to many people. I will try to remember that next time.

And thanks also to my amazing editor Emily Rodmell, who is able to make sense of the disjointed synopses I deliver her (how do you sort them out?) and patiently prods them into shape. I would not be the writer I am if it weren't for her.

As ever, eternal thanks to my Lord and Savior Jesus Christ, who has already won the victory. Thank you for hope and happy endings.

Dear Reader,

Family. Love them or hate them, like them or merely tolerate them, we are all influenced by our families. It's more than the genetic imprint they give us. Every interaction or lack of interaction influences who we are, molding and shaping us, or sending us running in the other direction.

In *Prince Incognito,* Alec can't remember who his family is. He can't even remember who *he* is! But even though he doesn't know he's a prince, he still behaves with integrity and honor, struggling toward uncovering the truth about where he came from.

In contrast, Lillian struggles to escape from her family. While her uncle and parents are motivated by greed and pride, Lily refuses to be a part of their plans. In spite of her background, Lily chooses to act with integrity and honor. And so, though their families are pitted against one another, Alec and Lily are drawn together by faith and the love that blossoms between them.

Of course, the Lydian royal family is still missing one member. Please look for the next book in the RECLAIMING THE CROWN series, *The Missing Monarch,* a September 2012 Love Inspired Suspense release, which follows the story of Thaddeus, the heir to the Lydian throne.

No matter where you came from or what your family was like, I pray you'll be encouraged by Alec and Lily's story. Are you trying to sort out where you came from? Or are you running from a family whose choices are contrary to your faith? Know that, no matter what your family is like, you have a heavenly Father who loves you, who will see you through all the challenges ahead and bring you to the happy ending you long for.

In Him,
Rachelle

Questions for Discussion

1. As his story opens, Alec has the impression that something isn't quite right. He feels out of place, but more than that, he suspects something is wrong. Have you ever had a similar feeling? What caused it? How did you respond?

2. From the moment Lillian sees the injured soldier, she feels like she needs to help him. How do you feel about her response? Do you agree with her decision to bring the injured man to her parents' boat? What might she have done differently under the circumstances? What would you have done?

3. Sandra Bardici seems quite interested in learning the identity of the soldier on their boat. As we learn much later in the story, she's been conspiring with her brother-in-law. Why do you think she was so interested in figuring out who Alec was? Do you think she recognized him and alerted David?

4. Alec repeatedly rescues Lily, even though he doesn't know who he is or why she's being threatened. What do his actions reveal about

his character? Why do you think he chose to do what he did?

5. From very early on in her adventure, Lily decides to ally herself with a man she doesn't know. What factors prompted her decision? Do you think she made the right choices?

6. Do you think Titus dropped his canteen on purpose? Why or why not?

7. As Alec realizes who he is and remembers what has happened, he feels a burning need to try to help his family, but at the same time there is little he can doing without risking getting caught. Have you ever wanted to help your loved ones, but felt hampered by circumstances? How did you overcome the constraints of your situation? How does Alec overcome the obstacles before him?

8. When Lily learns that the man she's falling in love with is really a prince, she tries unsuccessfully to quash her feelings. Do you think a person's station in life should influence how you feel about them? Have you ever had a friendship stifled by socioeconomic factors? Do you think this is how God intends for people to live?

9. With no money of her own, Lily has to rely on Alec's generosity. Have you ever had to accept something, knowing you might not get the chance to pay the giver back? How did you respond? How did that experience influence your future decisions?

10. As Alec and Lily debate whether to turn back, Lily says, "I'd rather die chasing a dream than giving up." Do you think it matters which way a person is headed when they die? What does Lily's statement reveal about her faith? Where was Jesus Christ headed when He died? Does His death influence the way you live your life?

11. If Alec and Lily had given up one ridge earlier, they would never have known an oasis lay just beyond them. Have you ever felt like giving up? What kept you going? Have you reached an oasis, or are you still trudging?

12. When Lily looks back at her footprints in the sand, she's reminded that God has carried her through all her trials, and even literally carried her in Alec's arms. Look back at the footprints along the path you've been walking. Can you see the places where God has carried you? Do your footprints dance in tandem with God's, or are there scuffle marks where you've been

fighting God's plans for your life? How does Lily's journey encourage you on your journey?

13. When David Bardici taunts Alec in the dungeon, he tells Alec he's failed his family and failed God. Do your enemies ever whisper similar taunts in your ears? How did Alec respond? Can you sort out the truth from the lies you've heard whispered?

14. When Lily realizes she needs the maid's key to get into her uncle's office, she refuses to steal it or to lie to the woman to get it. Instead, she's honest with the woman and politely asks to borrow it. Do you think God rewards those who choose to do the right thing? Is it ever okay to steal or lie?

15. Alec has served alongside his fellow soldiers. When he arrives with orders for General Bardici to step down, his fellow men immediately recognize his authority. Why do you think they respect him? How does your behavior influence the way others treat you? Do your actions reflect your faith in Christ and accurately represent the God you serve? What steps can you take to represent Christ in your daily life?

LARGER-PRINT BOOKS!

**GET 2 FREE
LARGER-PRINT NOVELS
PLUS 2 FREE
MYSTERY GIFTS**

Love Inspired®

SUSPENSE
RIVETING INSPIRATIONAL ROMANCE

Larger-print novels are now available...

LARGER-PRINT BOOKS!

GET 2 FREE LARGER-PRINT NOVELS PLUS 2 FREE MYSTERY GIFTS

Love Inspired

Larger-print novels are now available...